"With its warm and relatable cast of characters, *Blest Be the Tie* offers up parables of community and faith that feel instantly familiar and welcoming. White's collection of vignettes illuminates the Christian values and plain graces that unite, reconcile, and bring both healing and understanding."

—David Williams, author of *When the English Fall*

"When I first began reading *Blest Be the Tie*, I thought, 'I know these people.' As I continued reading, I thought, 'I am these people!' White takes what is common in all of us—our frailties, shortcomings, and wounds as well as our beauty, strength, and possibilities—and weaves together stories of community. Not only do we see ourselves, but we see the possibility of redeemed relationships and hopeful community that is a taste of 'on earth as it is in heaven.'"

—Joanne Lindstrom, Associate Professor of Ministry, McCormick Theological Seminary, Chicago

"White's beautifully written *Blest Be the Tie* are stories told with gentle humor and a tender touch. The author reveals a deep love for Scripture and a great confidence in its capacity to surprise us and to transform even the most demanding of our circumstances. These stories draw the reader in and leave us changed."

—Ian Adams, chaplain, Ridley Hall, Cambridge

"White is well familiar with pastoral ministry, and she shares congregational stories from Pastor Bob's Presbyterian church in the North Country in upstate New York. . . . White has created a caring, diverse, and integrated community of faith, and has given readers a vacation from their own lives and churches as they immerse themselves in the lives of Pastor Bob and his flock. Using poetic and descriptive language, White does not just tell stories; she paints rich pictures and shares complex emotions. . . . I was moved to tears often, and I laughed out loud several times. Reading this book made me want to be a better pastor—maybe as good as Pastor Bob, or maybe even, in my dreams, as accomplished and understanding as White herself. This is a diverting, engrossing, and pleasurable read."

—Laurie McKnight, spiritual care professional

D1525655

Blest Be the Tie

[signature] Eph. 4:32

Blest Be the Tie

—— *Fables of Faith from the Far North* ——

Joann White

RESOURCE *Publications* • Eugene, Oregon

BLEST BE THE TIE
Fables of Faith from the Far North

Resource Publications
An Imprint of Wipf and Stock Publishers
199 W. 8th Ave., Suite 3
Eugene, OR 97401

www.wipfandstock.com

PAPERBACK ISBN: 978-1-6667-0216-3
HARDCOVER ISBN: 978-1-6667-0217-0
EBOOK ISBN: 978-1-6667-0218-7

06/08/21

For Duane, who hikes mountains, plays music,
and edits copy with tenacity and love;

and for the churches that I have been blessed to serve:

Lincoln Park Presbyterian Church of Chicago, Illinois
Westminster Presbyterian Church of Wilmington, Delaware
Morton Grove Community Church of Morton Grove, Illinois
First Presbyterian Church of Saranac Lake, New York

"Blest Be the Tie That Binds"

—John Fawcett, 1782

Blest be the tie that binds
our hearts in Christian love;
the fellowship of kindred minds
is like to that above.

Before our Father's throne
we pour our ardent prayers;
our fears, our hopes, our aims are one,
our comforts and our cares.

We share our mutual woes,
our mutual burdens bear,
and often for each other flows
the sympathizing tear.

When we are called to part,
it gives us inward pain;
but we shall still be joined in heart,
and hope to meet again.

This glorious hope revives
our courage by the way;
while each in expectation lives
and waits to see the day.

From sorrow, toil, and pain,
and sin, we shall be free;
and perfect love and friendship reign
through all eternity.

Contents

1

Come Out!

Jesus cried with a loud voice, "Lazarus, come out!" The dead man came out, his hands and feet bound with strips of cloth, and his face wrapped in a cloth. Jesus said to them, "Unbind him, and let him go."

—JOHN 11:43B–44

M ost folks knew Tubby Mitchell. He ran the automotive shop and could tell what was wrong with your car just by listening to the engine. He was honest, too, stood by his repairs, and charged a fair price. The Mitchells had lived in the village even before there was a village. Tubby was raised by his grandfather, an Akwesasne Mohawk trapper and guide who knew every lake and trail in the mountains. Maybe that's where Tubby got his love of fishing. The Mitchells had a camp, not a fancy Great Camp, just a simple, year-round cabin on the lake with a screened porch, a big wood stove, and a little patch of green lawn out front. Tubby's wife Irene once told Pastor Bob that Tubby's real name was Tionatakwente, but no one other than Irene ever called him that. "Tionatakwente!"

Tubby and Irene had a boy. He was the spitting image of his dad, with dark hair and high cheekbones from his Mohawk heritage. Those two—Tubby and the boy—did just about everything together. They played basketball and worked on cars. They kept the yard neat for Irene, using an old-fashioned push mower to cut the grass. But what Tubby and the boy really liked to do was fish. In winter, they'd haul an old shanty out on the ice as soon as it got thick enough to bear their weight. They'd sit out there on Sunday afternoons after church, catching fish and listening to football on the radio. Irene would pack them lunch—ham sandwiches, apple pie, and a Thermos full of hot, black coffee for Tubby.

By the time the ice went out, Tubby and the boy would be ready for fly-fishing. The two of them in their hip waders, rods in hand, working the west branch of the Ausable River, were a study in rugged elegance. The strong flick of a wrist would send the fishing line humming in s-shaped waves above the surface of the water. A well-timed pause landed the fly with precision and barely a ripple. All summer long, they would row a guideboat across the upper lake, testing the waters of favorite fishing holes. Tubby was never prouder than the day he and the boy got their picture in the *Little City News*. There they were on the front page, grinning from ear to ear, each of them holding a big, largemouth bass out in front of them. The caption below the picture said, "Like father, like son." Tubby carried that picture in his wallet like it was a thousand-dollar bill.

When that boy was killed in Iraq, the whole town turned out for his funeral. Ernie Leduc had to set up extra folding chairs in the back of the Presbyterian Church, and all the girls wept over his flag-draped coffin. Even Pastor Bob took it hard, his voice shaking as he read, "I am the resurrection and the life. Those who believe in me, even though they die, will live, and everyone who lives and believes in me will never die." It was a hard day.

Tubby was never quite the same after he lost that boy. It was as if a light had gone out inside him. Down at the automotive shop, they noticed that Tubby stopped whistling. He gave up singing in the church choir, and folks had to make do without a tenor. What troubled Irene most, though, was that Tubby wouldn't fish anymore. She'd set out his gear, pack him a lunch, and fill the Thermos with hot coffee, but it would sit by the door all day long, untouched. It was unnatural.

Irene went to see Pastor Bob for advice. He listened close and nodded his head, and then he told her, "Irene, healing takes time. For some folks, it can take a very long time. We just have to trust that God is with Tubby. The Lord will call him out when the time is right."

Well, that didn't sound like very good advice to Irene. Healing may take time, but Pastor Bob didn't have to live with Tubby with his lights turned down low, did he? So, Irene went home and signed them up for a grief group. She dragged Tubby out monthly to the Family Bereavement Circle, and she bought books about the "six stages of grief" and "grief recovery" and the "mystery of grief" and "good grief." Irene felt a whole lot better, but Tubby just seemed the same.

One day, as they were on their way home from one of those meetings, Tubby gave Irene's hand a squeeze and said, "I know Todd is dead, Irene. I know he was a good boy and the Lord has taken him home, but I've got a hole in my heart that won't stop hurting. That's just the way it is." Irene's eyes filled with tears. She squeezed Tubby's hand back, and she decided right then and there to stop making Tubby go to meetings and circles.

When Tubby neared retirement and began to cut back his hours at the automotive shop, Irene hoped he would start fishing again. But Tubby didn't. He read the paper and looked out at the lake. He puttered about the house and took up gardening. He volunteered at the soup kitchen. Irene knew Tubby still carried that newspaper clipping of him and the boy because, every once in a while, she would catch him looking at it with a fierce intensity, as if he were trying to remember every detail of that day, every little thing about his boy.

One year, it got hot early. It was only the third week of June and the thermometer was hitting seventy degrees. Everyone agreed it was global warming. Tubby was out giving the yard the first mowing of the season with his old push mower, sweating and swatting at the black flies, when he got a peculiar sensation. He felt like someone was watching him. Tubby stopped and hauled out a bandanna to mop his brow. He looked right and left. Out of the corner of his eye, Tubby caught a flicker of motion. Two small feet in ratty sneakers were peeking out from under the big mountain laurel at the corner of the yard. Huh! Tubby had a visitor.

"Why don't you get out here and let me take a look at you?" Tubby asked.

Out popped a small boy, followed by a beat-up bicycle. The boy had a funny symmetry about him. He had scabs on both knees. He was missing both front teeth. He had carroty red hair that stuck out all over, and he was completely covered with freckles.

"What's your name?" Tubby asked.

A squeaky little voice answered, "Jackie Carl. What's *your* name?"

"Well, it's Tubby Mitchell."

This seemed to surprise Jackie Carl a bit because he next wanted to know, "What kind of a name is Tubby?"

Well, Tubby wasn't about to explain that his real name was Tionatak-wente, so he asked right back, "What kind of a name is Jackie Carl?"

At this, the squeaky little voice piped back, "It's the name my Daddy gave me before he went to prison. How old are you?"

Tubby felt like this was getting a little too personal. "Old enough," he answered, "How old are *you*?"

"Six," Jackie Carl answered. Then, gathering up all his courage, the little boy pointed to the antique mower and asked, "What's that?"

And at that, Tubby did something that he hadn't done in a very long time. He laughed. "That, my young friend, is a lawn mower."

Jackie Carl just looked at the mower in disbelief, like it was an outer-space oddity left behind by aliens.

"What's *that*?" Tubby asked, pointing to the boy's bike.

"This," the squeaky voice answered, "is the fastest bike in the world. Do you want to race?" Jackie Carl rang the bike's bell, just to show he meant business.

Tubby checked out the bike. It was a girl's bike that looked about thirty years old, white, with a banana seat, chopper handlebars, and a wicker basket out front that was covered with purple, plastic flowers and Hello Kitty stickers. The bike was much too large for the very little boy. Tubby laughed a second time that day and answered, "I'm retired from racing. Where'd you come from, anyway?"

"My mom sent me here for a summer vacation," Jackie Carl said. "My granny lives there." The boy pointed down across the road to the Underhill Farm.

"Ah," Tubby said thoughtfully, "I see. Who's taking the vacation, you or your mom?"

Jackie Carl answered truthfully, "I guess we both are. What do you like to do?"

Before Tubby knew what he was doing, he found himself saying, "Fishing. Fishing is what I like to do best."

This prompted a big smile from the little guy. "Me, too!" he said, and Jackie Carl looked at Tubby expectantly, as if an invitation to fish would naturally follow.

But there was no invitation, only an awkward silence. Tubby looked down at his old push mower, and he felt relieved when he heard Ruth Underhill calling from her front porch, "Jackie Carl, you stop bothering the neighbors!"

"That's my granny," the little voice said as he peddled away. "Bye, Tubby!"

The next morning early, as Tubby Mitchell sat drinking black coffee and reading the paper, he heard something that made him smile. A little voice was yelling out in the front yard, "Tubby Mitchell, come out!"

Irene came out of the kitchen, wiping her hands on a dishtowel. "What in the world is that?" she wanted to know.

Tubby glanced over the top of his paper and said, "I expect that's Jackie Carl, Ruth Underhill's grandson."

And as if on cue, the boy's high-pitched voice shouted again, "Tubby Mitchell, come out!"

Irene looked from Tubby to the door and said, "Tubby, aren't you going to get up and answer him?"

Tubby folded his paper, got up, and walked over to the front door. He swung it open and saw Jackie Carl there in the yard on his bike. The boy had an old tackle box crammed into the bike's basket, and Tubby saw that he had made himself a fishing pole from a green branch. "Well, good morning, Jackie Carl," Tubby said, but Jackie Carl wasn't looking to exchange pleasantries.

"Tubby Mitchell," he squeaked, "come out. I want you to take me fishing. My granny said you could."

"Oh, she did, did she?" Tubby's smile faded, and he froze in the door for a few moments.

It was Irene who broke the silence as she stood behind her husband and placed a hand on his shoulder. "Tionatakwente, you know it wouldn't hurt you to give that poor boy a morning of your time."

As Tubby stood there looking at the little boy with his too-big bike, carroty hair, freckles, and homemade fishing pole, Tubby felt funny. He put his hand over his heart, and it seemed as if something woke up and turned over inside there, something that had been sleeping for a very, very long time. Tubby felt an odd lump in his throat, and when he turned to look at Irene, he saw that she was crying.

Tubby gave a little wave to the boy and said, "Very well, Jackie Carl. I'll be right out." He gathered his gear, and Irene made them a picnic, and then Tubby and Jackie Carl went fishing. It was the first of many trips that they made together that summer.

One day, as Irene was hanging out the laundry and Tubby was deadheading flowers in the yard, Irene heard something. At first, she wasn't sure that she had really heard it, so she stopped with a clothespin in her mouth and held her breath. It was soft and low, but clear, and as Irene listened, it grew stronger. Tubby was whistling. When the fall rolled around, Tubby surprised everyone at the Presbyterian Church by showing up for choir practice on Wednesday evenings. The altos were all relieved that one of them wouldn't have to try to sing tenor any more.

After church one day, as Tubby swapped fishing stories with the men, Pastor Bob smiled at Irene and waved her over. "Irene, I see that the Lord has finally called Tubby to come out." They looked over at Tubby, holding his hands up in front of him to show the size of the last fish that he had caught, and Irene could see that the light, which had gone out in Tubby with the death of their boy, was once again glowing within him.

"Pastor Bob," Irene said, "do you ever think about what Jesus looked like?"

Pastor Bob's brow wrinkled a little bit with thought. "I'm not sure where you're going with that, Irene."

"Well, I've been thinking lately that sometimes Jesus can sneak up on you. He can really surprise you."

"Uh-huh," Pastor Bob nodded along. "Say more, Irene."

She did. "Sometimes, Jesus can look an awful lot like a little boy with a squeaky voice, scabby knees, red hair, freckles, and a homemade fishing pole."

As Pastor Bob began to chew on that bit of wisdom, Irene collected her husband and headed home. They say that when the lakes ice over, Tubby and Jackie Carl have big plans for a weekend of ice fishing.

2

No Longer Strangers

"For he is our peace; in his flesh he has made both groups
into one and has broken down the dividing wall, that is,
the hostility between us."

—EPHESIANS 2:14

When young Pastor Bob first came to the Presbyterian Church, he noticed a certain chill in the air on Sunday mornings, even on warm
summer days when the old sanctuary was hot and steamy enough to poach
an egg. At first, he thought it was just your typical Presbyterian frozen-
chosen sort of vibe, but that chilly feeling just didn't go away. In fact, the
more he noticed it, the worse it seemed to feel, especially during that time
in the service when everyone shared the peace of Christ, turning to their
neighbors with hugs and handshakes and hellos.

One Sunday, Pastor Bob decided to conduct an experiment. He
launched into his usual invitation: "Our Lord Jesus taught, 'Peace I give
to you, my peace I leave with you; not as the world gives do I give to you.
Let not your hearts be troubled, neither let them be afraid.' Let's greet one
another with the peace of Christ." When folks got up to pass the peace,
though, instead of rushing down into the congregation to greet folks, Bob
stayed up on the chancel, where he could get a good look at the whole assembly. He smiled and waved to people; he even flashed some peace signs.

Now, as Pastor Bob looked out over his little flock, he noticed that two
people weren't passing the peace at all. Maybelle Howard, way up front by
the baptismal font, and Lenore Claiborne, way back on the other side of
the sanctuary in the very last pew, were both rooted in their seats, staring

straight ahead, not making eye contact with any of their neighbors. And their neighbors, perhaps warned off by years of non-response, just let them be. It was like each woman had a barrier around her, a partition put up to keep someone out. Just looking at the icy wall those two had built around themselves gave Pastor Bob the shivers. "Peace be with you, indeed," he thought. "I've got my work cut out for me, don't I?"

After the service, as Pastor Bob greeted people in the narthex, he paid special attention as first Maybelle and then Lenore came down the line. He noticed that the women were about the same age, about the age his mother would have been if she were still living.

"Nice day, Maybelle," Pastor Bob said, reaching out to shake her hand.

"It *is* a nice day, Pastor," Maybelle responded in an overly loud voice before leaning in to whisper in Bob's ear, "though some people wouldn't know a nice day if it hit them upside the head."

Before he could even think of a response, Maybelle was off, and there was Lenore, right in front of him. "Nice day, Lenore," Pastor Bob tried.

But Lenore gave him a hard look and said, "Sure, it's a nice day, as long as you're not hoping to make goulash."

Pastor Bob couldn't think of much to say in response to that, so he lamely offered, "I *love* goulash," but Lenore just sniffed and stormed off to the parking lot. Right then, Bob decided that he had indeed identified the source of his Sunday shivers. "Lord, have mercy," he prayed, watching Maybelle and Lenore climb into their cars and roar off in opposite directions.

Small-town folks love to talk. It didn't take Pastor Bob more than a few days to get to the bottom of the wall that seemed to divide the two women. It started when Maybelle gave birth to her third child. It was a tough birth—the baby almost died—and Maybelle had to stay in the hospital for a whole week. The women of the church stepped forward to prepare meals for the Howard family while Maybelle rested and recovered.

Lenore had been the first to arrive at the Howard door with a Crock-Pot full of her prize-winning goulash—the kind with the elbow macaroni, chunky ground beef, tomatoes, and onion. Lenore swore that the family was so hungry—and her goulash was so good—that they were getting ready to eat it right out of the crock, standing around with spoons in their hands as she said her goodbyes and headed out the door.

Now, the conflict between the two women seems to have erupted over what happened next. Lenore insists that she never got her Crock-Pot back. That's right—Maybelle Howard as good as stole it, keeping it for herself, probably uses it every Sunday. But Maybelle maintains that she gave it back, brought it to church one Sunday with a nice note of thanks taped to the top, liberally sealed with a host of smiley-face stickers from her children. Maybelle specifically remembered bringing the Crock-Pot back because at the same time she had also returned the backup coffee urn that she had borrowed from the church for the baby's shower. She had to make repeat trips from her car into the church in her weakened state, first with the Crock-Pot and then with the big coffee pot. Who could forget that? It was a wonder that she had survived the ordeal.

When Maybelle heard through the grapevine that Lenore never got her Crock-Pot back, she felt terrible. She even went out and bought Lenore a new one. Maybelle left it on Lenore's doorstep with all the ingredients that she might need to make another delicious pot of goulash. But, the very next day, Maybelle found the brand new one on her own front porch, with all the goulash ingredients mashed up inside and a terse note that said, "I liked my old pot just fine. Give it back."

No matter how hard folks at church worked to reconcile Maybelle and Lenore, the damage had been done—the wall had been built, and it was not coming down. For twenty years now, they had refused to speak to one another or even be in the same room. Through intermediaries, they had somehow worked out an alternating calendar of attendance at church social events so that they wouldn't have to contend with one another. The only problem, of course, was Sunday morning and the passing of the peace. Neither woman would forego Sunday worship, so they resolved to just sit tight during the peace and wait for it to be over. Each year only seemed to make the wall between the women more impenetrable, and everyone else had long since given up on trying to build a bridge where none was clearly wanted.

Pastor Bob saw that he had before him perhaps the most monumental challenge of his young ministerial career. He couldn't wait to be the great peacemaker. Pastor Bob began with a sermon series on forgiveness, preaching for a month about Jesus saying that we should turn the other cheek, walk the extra mile, love our enemies, and forgive seventy-seven times. Next, Pastor Bob tried preaching on reconciliation. Week after week, he talked about Jacob finally renewing his relationship with Esau, and Joseph reuniting with his rascally brothers after they sold him into slavery, and Jesus sharing a fish breakfast with Peter, who had denied him three times. Finally, Pastor Bob launched into a sermon series on the radical love that the apostle Paul saw in the early church—Jews and Gentiles, men and women, slaves and freeborn, rich and poor, all brought together through the blood of Christ into a wonderful, welcoming community. Pastor Bob preached his young heart out, week after week, month after month.

The whole church got caught up in the gospel spirit. More folks than ever before walked in the CROP Hunger Walk. The food-pantry basket was overflowing with donations. The church life committee started a new program to welcome in strangers, and ten new people joined the church! But Maybelle and Lenore, they stayed the same, each glued to her pew on Sunday morning, staring straight ahead and not passing the peace. Eventually, Pastor Bob went back to preaching from the lectionary. He decided that the only person who could reconcile Maybelle and Lenore was Jesus, and even the prince of peace might find it a challenge. "Lord Jesus," he prayed, "I'm handing this one off to you. Good luck, boss."

The two women might have gone to their graves feeling enmity for one another if the old coffee urn hadn't blown up one Sunday morning, right in the middle of coffee hour. One moment it was humming on the counter, its red brew light casting a reassuring glow to all the java junkies, and the next moment it was like a creature possessed. The cord began to buzz and smoke. Sparks started shooting out of the base, and then while everyone looked on in horror, it burst into flames just before Pastor Bob could assault it with the fire extinguisher. The kids are still talking about that Sunday. Once the smoke cleared, folks got over their shock and began to laugh about it. They figured that the urn had been used every Sunday for at least twenty years, and it was about time that it had a meltdown.

It wasn't until later in the week, when Pastor Bob went in search of the backup coffee urn, that he made his discovery. As Bob lifted the urn down from the top of the kitchen pantry, he noticed something on the shelf, way back behind it. It had the short, stout, reassuring dimensions of a Crock-Pot, and as Bob climbed up higher to get a good look, he noticed that it had a note taped on top, all covered with bright, cheerful smiley faces. It was very dusty. Pastor Bob couldn't believe his eyes. After all these years, Lenore Claiborne's beloved, long-lost Crock-Pot had been found. It was a miracle. "Thank you, Jesus!" Pastor Bob said as he lifted the cherished vessel down from the back of the pantry as if it were the Holy Grail and carried it to his office to pray about what to do next.

Later, just before quitting time, Pastor Bob pulled a sheet of paper out of his desk drawer and wrote a simple note. "Dear Lenore, I found this

Crock-Pot on the top shelf of the kitchen pantry, behind the backup coffee urn. I believe it belongs to you. I'm praying for you. My love to you in Christ, Pastor Bob." Bob started to fold up the note, but he stopped and added a verse from Paul's letter to the church in Ephesus, writing, "For Jesus is our peace; in his flesh he has made both groups into one and has broken down the dividing wall, that is the hostility between us." For good measure, Pastor Bob added a smiley face, too.

On his way home, Pastor Bob made two stops. First, he swung by Green's Grocery and picked up all the ingredients to make goulash. Then, he drove over to Lenore Claiborne's place and left the Crock-Pot, his note, and the goulash fixings on her porch where she later found it when she got home from her Weight Watchers meeting.

The following morning, remembering what they say about those who hesitate, Lenore Claiborne decided not to go into her shop. From memory, she made her prize-winning goulash for the first time in twenty years. She ferried her beloved Crock-Pot to the car and drove straight to Maybelle Howard's house. The two women spent the day crying and eating goulash, catching up and thanking God for breaking down the dividing wall between them.

The next Sunday when Pastor Bob entered the sanctuary, he noticed that there was a special energy buzzing about, a liveliness unlike that usual Presbyterian, frozen-chosen vibe. It wasn't until it came time to pass the peace that Bob saw exactly what had warmed people's hearts and loosened their tongues. Up front by the baptismal font sat Lenore Claiborne and Maybelle Howard, happy, smiling, side by side, like the best of friends. "Let's greet one another with the peace of Christ," Bob invited, and for the first time in twenty years, Lenore and Maybelle got out of the pew, smiled at their neighbors, and even hugged one another.

After church, as Pastor Bob greeted folks in the narthex, Lenore and Maybelle came through the line together, looking like it was just as natural as it could be. Maybelle spoke up first, "Pastor Bob, we want you and Marge to come eat Sunday dinner with us after coffee fellowship."

Bob, looking from Maybelle to Lenore, smiled and said, "Sounds great! What's for dinner, ladies?"

It was Lenore who answered, "I hear you *love* goulash. How about it, Pastor Bob?"

And later that day, for the second time in twenty years, Lenore Claiborne made her prize-winning goulash. Lenore, Maybelle, Pastor Bob, and Marge ate every bite.

3

Great Things

"For the Mighty One has done great things for me,
and holy is his name."

—Luke 1:49

Pastor Bob turned out the lights and locked the doors. He felt the over-
tired peace and contentment that comes to the pastors of small churches
after the last carol has been sung on Christmas Eve. As his boots squeaked
across the snow to his car, he half sang, half hummed under his breath,
"Silent night, holy night, all is calm, all is bright." Bob's wife Marge and
son Paul had gone ahead home, but Bob had one more stop. Charlie and
Annette Miller had welcomed a baby boy earlier that evening, and Pastor
Bob wanted to visit the newest member of his flock.

Now, Charlie and Annette had just sent their last child off to college and
were settling into their newly empty nest when they got the unexpected news
that a baby was on the way. Once the couple had gotten over the shock, they
warmed up to the idea. They joked that they were older and wiser now, with
more time and patience to give a child. Over the last nine months, Pastor
Bob had looked down from the pulpit on Sunday mornings to see Charlie
and Annette, side by side, joyful, holding hands, as if the surprise of a coming child had rekindled their love and happiness. But that evening, when
Pastor Bob cleared the church answering machine of messages, he had heard
Charlie's voice, sounding shaky and overwhelmed. "Bob, it's me, Charlie. The
baby's here. We're at the hospital." As Bob replayed the message, he could
hear from his voice that Charlie needed a pastor and a friend.

The lighting was soft and low in the birthing suite at the hospital. Annette was sound asleep. Her face had that blotchy, swollen look that only

comes after lots of crying. Charlie was in a rocker, looking weary. Cradled in his arms was a small bundle. A blue, knit cap proclaimed, "It's a boy." Bob pulled over a chair and sat down. "Charlie," Bob said, "you look like you could use a break. Why don't you let me hold my littlest lamb?" Reluctantly, Charlie passed over the baby.

Bob looked down into the little face. He saw that it was very round. The eyes, though closed, had a beautiful almond shape. The nose was broad. The chin was tiny. A little, fat pink tongue poked out between rosebud lips. Bob looked from the infant to Charlie, who finally broke his silence. "Down syndrome. What do you think, Bob?"

Bob looked back at the baby and sighed. The child's eyes flew open and peered up directly at him, intensely aware, bright, and curious. Suddenly, Bob had the feeling that the Holy Spirit was about to tap him on the shoulder. He smiled down at the baby and said, "Charlie, I think your boy is the most beautiful child I've ever seen."

If Pastor Bob had any worries that the church would be less than welcoming to Charles Miller II, or Junior as his parents called him, they soon vanished. The child was so sweet and pleasant that the nursery never lacked for volunteers. Folks claimed that they never felt so peaceful as they did when they held the little guy. Junior might have taken a little longer to learn to walk than most children, but once he found his feet, he never seemed to stop. His short fat legs were always chasing after others in the Shrove Tuesday pancake-relay race, and he became particularly adept at hiding when it came time to play sardines.

While other children aged up and out of the Sunday morning children's time, Junior didn't. Pastor Bob took to inviting not just the children but also those feeling a little childlike to join him at the front of the sanctuary. Up to the front Junior would troop, taking a quiet, respectful seat on the edge of the chancel behind all the little children.

When Junior finished school, Eugenia Bergstrom, the worship committee chairperson, let Bob know that she thought it was time for Junior to graduate from children's time, too. Bob thought about it. "Well, Eugenia," he finally said, "the Lord taught that if we want to enter the kingdom of heaven, we need to be like children. I guess Junior is a whole lot closer to heaven than most of us. I'm not inclined to mess with that. Are you?" The topic never came up again.

The year that Junior turned twenty, he moved to a group home. Charlie and Annette had retired, and even though it was hard for them to let go, they knew that it was time for their youngest child to leave the nest. Junior had a paying job out at the Underhill Dairy, where they said he could soothe skittish cows and horses. Junior had even struck up an unlikely friendship with the Underhill's mean and nasty brood sow Pigzilla. Pastor Bob noticed that Junior was a natural evangelist in his new home environment. It wasn't long before many of Junior's housemates were in church, taking up a whole pew at the front of the sanctuary where most of Bob's parishioners were reluctant to sit.

One Sunday worship, as Advent rolled on toward Christmas, Pastor Bob invited the children forward. As they gathered around Bob, they saw that he held in his hands an old-fashioned papier-mâché figure from the church's nativity scene, definitely feminine, kneeling, wearing a blue cloak, smiling beatifically. "Who can tell me whom I've brought for us to meet this morning?" Bob asked, holding up the figure.

Every little right hand shot up at once, soon followed by the universal chorus, "Mary! It's Mary!"

"Excellent!" laughed Pastor Bob before launching into the ancient story of Mary, the poor, unwed, teenage, peasant girl, who gave birth to the messiah. "Do you know what Mary teaches us?" Pastor Bob finished up. No hands shot up this time, but he could tell that every ear was listening. "Mary teaches us that God can do great things through us, even if we are poor and powerless and little in the eyes of the world. God can do great things through you."

As Pastor Bob reached out to hold hands and pray the children out, a soft man's voice asked from the edge of the circle, "Me, too, Pastor Bob? Can God do great things through me?" It was Junior, his eyes directly on Bob, intensely aware, bright and curious.

For a moment, Bob was back in that birthing suite, all those years ago, holding a tiny infant while the Holy Spirit tapped him on the shoulder. "Junior, I see God doing great things through you every day. Let's pray."

Later that week, Pastor Bob almost walked right into the short round form of Junior Miller. He was standing outside Bob's office, carefully inspecting all the flyers and photos tacked to the mission bulletin board. "Junior! What brings you here?"

"I want to do a great thing for the Lord, Pastor Bob. What's best?" Bob looked at the board. There was a sign-up for taking canned goods to the food pantry. There were snapshots of the church's vegetable plot in the community garden. Bob saw a picture of Tubby Mitchell smiling from behind the lunch counter of the Good News Café, an ecumenical outreach to hungry neighbors. The newsletter from the Crisis Care Nursery, in Mzuzu, Malawi, showed tiny HIV-positive babies peeping through mosquito nets. A big thank-you card from Marion Medical Mission featured a picture of an African village, with all the residents celebrating as clean water gushed from their new shallow well.

"Well, Junior, they're all great works, some close to home, some far away. I don't know if there is a best. Why don't you just listen to your heart? I'm sure the Lord will let you know how you can help." This seemed to make perfect sense to Junior, who nodded and continued his study of the bulletin board.

In the weeks and months that followed, Pastor Bob heard stories. Junior's heart must have been doing a lot of talking, and Junior must have been doing a lot of listening. Tubby Mitchell called one day to thank Bob for sending Junior over to the Good News Café. Tubby said that when Junior had told Ruth Underhill at the dairy all about the soup kitchen, she had decided to begin donating the dairy's eggs and milk that were nearing their expiration dates. "Our cup now overfloweth!" Tubby rejoiced.

Come springtime, Bob heard from the church's gardeners. Junior had come out with friends to help them plant. They sure had appreciated the extra hands, and even better, Junior hooked them up with a truckload of composted manure—beautiful, rich, organic stuff from the cows, horses, and Pigzilla. The beans, beets, and lettuce were practically jumping out of the ground, and a bumper harvest was expected. "Just wait until the folks at the food pantry see this!" they celebrated.

As the year continued, Bob heard story after story about Junior Miller. The young man was a living, breathing object lesson in how a caring heart and willing hands could make a difference.

Nothing, though, could have prepared Pastor Bob for what happened on the last Sunday of Advent. That year, as Bob invited the children and the childlike forward, he held the figurine of the shepherd from the church's nativity scene, youthful and barefoot, staff in hand, a lamb draped casually over his shoulders. As the children took their places, Bob noticed that Junior, in his usual spot on the edge of the chancel, was holding a cardboard box. Someone had used a lot of masking tape to cover it in brown paper and there were pictures pasted to the outside, which Bob recognized from the Marion Medical Mission flyers. In big letters, obviously written by Junior's short, fat fingers, were the words, "Shallow Well." Bob forgot all about the shepherd. "Junior, what's that you've got?"

"It's for the shallow well, Pastor Bob," Junior said as he handed over the box. The congregation made an "Awww!" noise, the kind of sound that folks make when they see kittens or puppies. But as Bob took the box, he noticed that it was surprisingly heavy. Junior smiled. "We all saved a dollar a day, our counselors, too, Mrs. Underhill, too! Count it, Pastor Bob! Count it!" Bob saw that Junior's friends in the front pew were smiling and nodding. One was already clapping with joyous anticipation. Ruth Underhill, who was sitting in the back of the church, yelled out, "Count it already, Bob."

Before Bob could even open his mouth, the children had stripped the paper from the box and pried the lid off as the congregation cheered them on. But as they dumped the contents out onto the carpet, everyone fell silent. It was, quite simply, the biggest wad of cash that Bob had ever beheld. Molly Hall, who was ten years old going on twenty-five, took charge of the count, quickly stacking bills and scribbling totals on an offering envelope. $1,000! $2,000! $3,000! When the last bill was counted, more than $4,000 was stacked neatly on the floor, enough to provide shallow wells for ten African villages.

Bob looked out in the pews at Charlie and Annette Miller, smiling, holding hands, tears streaming down their faces. They weren't the only ones crying. Bob reached up to touch his face, wet with tears that fell upon the shepherd figurine that still rested in his lap. An awed silence hovered over the church.

"Pastor Bob, what do you think?" It was Junior, his brow furrowed, clearly worried that all the tears meant that he had perhaps done something wrong. Pastor Bob looked from the shepherd in his lap to the round face of Junior Miller. He looked deep into those beautiful almond-shaped eyes, intensely aware, bright, and curious. Bob could feel the Holy Spirit, brushing him again with gentle wings.

"Well, Junior, I feel a lot like how that shepherd must have felt when he looked into the manger and saw the Messiah staring back at him. You are beautiful, and you have done a great thing, my friend."

At that, the whole congregation burst into spontaneous applause. As the children, led by Molly Hall, began tossing handfuls of money up into the air, Pastor Bob made Junior Miller stand up and take a humble bow.

4

Coming and Going

"While he was blessing them, he withdrew from them."

—LUKE 24:51A

As Bob greeted folks after the service, he had that familiar, tired and empty feeling that always made him aware that it really was time for a break. It was a little like the labored movements of a wind-up toy that had all but wound down, or the flat over-squeezed look of a toothpaste tube that was just as good as empty. Just one more day, then Bob and Marge would be off for a little rest and relaxation. They'd been saving to spend a romantic week in Quebec City, and Paul had been bundled off downstate for some fun with his cousins. Marge had been practicing her French, which was a good thing because although Bob knew his way around biblical Greek and Hebrew, he found the mumbled rhythms of the Quebecois to be indecipherable and intimidating, all at the same time. Bob planned to speak as little as possible in the coming week, and that suited both him and Marge just fine.

When Lenore Claiborne huffed her way to the front of the greeting line, Bob gave her plump hand a reassuring squeeze. "Lenore!" he smiled, "So good to worship with you today!"

Lenore didn't return the sentiment. Instead she held out her bulletin. It had been carefully folded to expose the brightly colored sheet of weekly announcements. "What's this?" Lenore wanted to know, tapping the page at the precise point where the words "Pastor Bob and Marge will be out of town" heralded the news of Bob's impending departure.

Although Bob had long ago learned that an occasional parishioner would always begrudge him time away, he was never able to completely quell that squirmy, guilty feeling that someone like Lenore could stir up inside him. He usually coped by adopting an obtuse and overly chipper air. "How good of you to notice, Lenore! Quebec City for us this year! A little culture, a little fine dining, a little *je ne sais quoi*. What do you think?"

Lenore's raised eyebrows told Bob that she was clearly unimpressed. She looked at Bob over the top of her glasses and said, "You have fun with the Frenchies, Bob, but if you think I'm telling *my* care concerns to a deacon of the month, you've got another think coming." Lenore stalked off to inspect the coffee hour treats before Bob could think of an appropriately chipper response.

The next day was a blur for Bob. Aware of his impending travels, everyone was eager for a little of his time. His calendar was blanketed with pastoral care appointments. Between visitors, Bob's secretary, Linda, peppered him with questions: "Who should give the honorarium to the supply preacher? Where is the cordless microphone? What's your emergency contact information?" And, "What should I do if one of your 'friends' comes by?" "Friends," of course, was the euphemism everyone at church used for the down-and-out neighbors who regularly came to see Bob for counsel or prayer or financial aid.

At quarter to five, as Bob bid farewell to his last appointment and was just beginning to think he was home free, the phone rang. It was Carol Burgess, the supply preacher. She was so glad to have caught him. She was having a busy week, and now that she was retired, she was out of the habit of writing liturgy. Surely Bob wouldn't mind preparing the Sunday service for her. Bob sighed and scribbled down Carol's lections. He then called Marge to say he'd be late, booted the computer back up, and got to work.

Around eight o'clock, as Bob drove home to a plate of cold chicken and a long night of packing, he wondered if it had been like this for Jesus before the ascension. Every painting Bob had ever seen of the glorious event depicted it in such hallowed hues. Jesus was always rising against puffy, white, cumulous clouds, surrounded by a heavenly host of cherubim and bright angels. Jesus's eyes were turned heavenward with a soft and dreamy expression. His countenance was serene and in control. One hand was half-extended in a gesture of casual blessing, as if it were an everyday occurrence to be swept up into heaven to take a seat at the right hand of God almighty. In one of Bob's favorite paintings, by some unknown sixteenth-century German artist, all that could be seen of Jesus were his feet. That's right, just the feet, no body, right up at the top of the canvas, poking out of the bottom of a voluminous robe and hovering just above the disciples' heads.

The disciples were always depicted in various states of reverence. In some paintings, they knelt with folded hands in an attitude of pious prayer. In others, the disciples were crowned with golden halos, looking up in adoration at their ascending Lord. In a few paintings, the disciples were all swoony, as if the mystery of Jesus rising to the Father were just too wonderful and holy to bear in an upright position.

But as Pastor Bob drove home that night, he had one of those lucid moments that sometimes come in ministry. It was one of those moments when he knew better. Bob suspected that, as Jesus ascended, the Lord probably cast a few rueful glances down, hoping all would be well with his friends. And the disciples, watching Jesus ascend, were probably a whole lot less reverent than they were anxious. Their hearts sank and their brows furrowed with worries about who would heal the sick, preach the good news, feed the hungry, and touch the local lepers. If Bob were a betting man, he'd lay good odds that more than a few hands had reached up in desperation to snatch at Jesus's robe. A few might have even done some jumping and grabbing. If he could look close, he might even see some scratch marks around those holy ankles that were bound for glory. In fact, if Bob were to paint the miraculous moment, he might color Jesus looking vaguely alarmed as he rose to the heavens with a determined disciple dangling from each foot.

As Bob pulled into the driveway, he wondered which had been harder, for Jesus to say goodbye or for the disciples to let go? Bob guessed that, in the end, the disciples and Jesus had all needed to trust that God had a plan for them and would equip them with what was needed, when it was needed, whether it was the Holy Spirit, the gift of proclamation, the peace that surpasses understanding, or a healthy dose of confidence.

Bob parked the car, checked the mailbox, and put his key in the front door. All Bob's deep theological musings evaporated as Marge threw open the door and purred in her silkiest tones, "*Ah, Robert! Viens voir mes estampes japonaises!*" Bob had just enough French to be able to decipher, "Bob! Come and see my etchings!" Vacation was officially under way.

In the week that Bob and Marge were gone, things went just fine at the church. Lenore Claiborne didn't have any pastoral care concerns after all, but she did hear that Heather Rodriguez had the flu and José and the kids were practically starving to death. So, Lenore fired up her infamous Crock-Pot and her convection oven. She made the Rodriguez family a batch of her prize-winning goulash, a loaf of sourdough bread, and a big pan of fudgy, chewy brownies, much to their delight.

The pilot light on the church's ancient hot-water heater went out mid-week. No amount of effort would get it relit. After much tinkering, Tubby Mitchell determined that he had to replace the thermocouple, a feat he was able to accomplish with only a modicum of swearing.

When Juice MacLeod stopped by the church on Friday, looking worn and frazzled and in need of a visit with his friend Bob, Linda invited him in and asked him to take a seat. She made Juice a cup of coffee, listened to his troubles, and told him she'd keep him in her prayers. Now Pastor Bob isn't the only one at church with a down-and-out friend.

On Sunday, the Rev. Carol Burgess preached the house down, even though she hadn't had much time for sermon preparation. When she finished, there was laughter and clapping and shouts of "Alleluia!" They say that even Eugenia Bergstrom, who frowns upon any form of demonstrative worship, said "Amen!" before clamping both hands over her mouth in dismay at her unruly outburst.

That week, God did, indeed, provide what was needed for those worried disciples. Yet, just as important, the folks down at the Presbyterian Church realized that they could do God's work, whether Pastor Bob was right there with them, or he was eating *foie gras* with Marge at *Le Pain Beni* in Old Quebec City.

And Pastor Bob? Let's just say he got his groove back. *Ooh là là!*

5

Doubt–full

He said to them, "Why are you frightened, and why
do doubts arise in your hearts?"

—LUKE 24:38

Most years, Pastor Bob led a confirmation class down at the Presbyterian Church, preparing youth for membership. They read scripture, did a service project, and learned the teachings of their Reformed tradition. It was always a joy for everyone when Pentecost arrived and the youth made their profession of faith, not just because the class was finally over but also because the young people had worked hard and grown in faith.

The year that Molly Hall was confirmed was memorable for Bob. Molly was thirteen going on thirty—bright, serious, and quick to tire of his jokes. By the end of the first confirmation lesson, Pastor Bob wondered if something was wrong with Molly. She seemed to roll her eyes at the slightest provocation. Although everyone knew that Pastor Bob's jokes were lame, out of common courtesy no one ever told him so to his face until Molly came along.

One evening as the confirmation students finished class and packed up, Molly stayed seated, her forehead creased, looking down at the study Bible in her lap. When the last student had left, Molly looked up. "Pastor Bob, does everyone who joins the church believe in the resurrection?"

Pastor Bob sat up a little straighter and pushed his eyeglasses back up on the bridge of his nose. "Well, Molly, that's a big question. I think folks who worship here affirm the resurrection, but they might not all share the same understanding of what happened on that first Easter Sunday."

The furrow between Molly's eyes deepened. "What's that supposed to mean?"

Pastor Bob suddenly noticed that it was a little warm in the room. Beads of sweat broke out on his brow. "Well, Molly, some people are literalists, but other people are more metaphorical."

The furrow on Molly's forehead grew deeper still. "Meta-huh?" Molly tried again, "Pastor Bob, what about you? Do you believe in the resurrection?"

At that, Pastor Bob did something that Molly was not expecting. He smiled and relaxed. "Absolutely!" he said, thumping his hand on the table. "I see Jesus on a regular basis."

At first Molly's mouth dropped open in disbelief, and then she snorted and rolled her eyes. Slamming her study Bible shut, she said, "Yeah, right, Pastor Bob. That's a good one. Thanks a lot."

Molly stood up to leave, but Pastor Bob stopped her. "Molly, sounds like you are struggling with doubt. You know, Jesus has been appearing to doubtful people for thousands of years. Just think about those disciples on that first Easter evening. I'm willing to bet that Jesus will make an appearance for you." The furrow was now gone from Molly's forehead; instead, her eyebrows were raised with skepticism.

"How about a special confirmation assignment, Molly? Next week is spring break. Why don't you come spend a day with me here at the church, and we'll see if we run into the risen Lord?"

Now, Molly could think of many things that she would rather do than spend a day of her vacation with Pastor Bob, but she was intrigued by the possibility of bumping into Jesus in the sacristy—or maybe just proving Pastor Bob dead wrong. "You're on, Pastor Bob. Tuesday!" Molly said as she stomped out the door.

At nine on Tuesday morning, Molly appeared in the doorway to Pastor Bob's study. He noticed that she had a digital camera, an old-fashioned tape recorder, and a notebook, the kind that kids use in school. "Molly, I see that you are well prepared," Bob said as he gathered up his communion kit and Bible. "Keep your coat on. We're heading out to Sunny Vue."

Molly's face fell as they walked toward the car. "Sunny Vue Nursing Home? My great-granny lives there. It smells."

"Really? I never noticed," Bob said, opening the car door, "Well, I think we have a good chance of seeing Jesus there. Shall we hold our noses and check it out?"

Molly sulked the whole way to Sunny Vue, and her mood did not improve when they arrived and went directly to her great-grandmother's room. "Pastor Bob!" Molly hissed at him. "If I want to visit my great-granny, I can do it with my mother. Just look at her. She won't even know that we're here."

Sure enough, Molly's great-grandmother just sat and stared, not even acknowledging their presence. While Pastor Bob made one-sided small talk, all about Holy Week and book studies and prayer groups, Molly fumed and squirmed in her chair. She opened up her notebook and wrote in big, bold, capital letters: "JESUS IS NOT AT SUNNY VUE."

After a while, Pastor Bob got out his communion kit and said, "Let's share the Lord's Supper." Molly reluctantly dragged her chair over. She took a few pictures of the bread and grape juice perched on Pastor Bob's lap, and she turned on her tape recorder, just for good measure. Molly's great-granny just sat and stared as if they were invisible. They bowed their heads, and when Pastor Bob said, "The Lord be with you," Molly automatically answered, "And also with you."

Much to Molly's surprise, she realized that she wasn't the only person responding to Pastor Bob's liturgy. For the first time in years, Molly heard her great-granny speak: "And also with you . . . We lift them to the Lord . . . It is right to give our thanks and praise."

When they got to the Lord's Prayer, Molly sat in awed silence while Pastor Bob and her great-grandmother prayed, "Our Father, who art in heaven." It wasn't as if her great-granny had suddenly tuned into their presence and was communing with them; rather, it was as if someone else was there in the room with them, some holy presence that spanned that unbridgeable gap and spoke to Molly's great-granny in ways that they could not.

As they drove back to the church, Pastor Bob saw that Molly was busy scratching away in her notebook, but when he tried to sneak a peek, she snapped it shut. "Mind your own beeswax, Pastor Bob."

Back at the church, Molly wanted to know, "What's next?"

"Well," Pastor Bob said, "I've got to do some reading to prepare for my sermon on Sunday. Why don't you take a look around here and see what you turn up? Every once in a while, Jesus even comes to church." Molly rolled her eyes, and Pastor Bob settled into the pastor's study with a big pile of books.

Out in the hallway now, Molly sighed, closed her eyes, and listened. The first thing she heard was a funny noise, "Scrrrtch, scrrrtch, scrrrtch."

Molly switched the tape recorder on and followed the sound to the kitchen. There, she saw Irene Mitchell crouched on her hands and knees, facing into a corner. How strange!

"Mrs. Mitchell, what are you doing?"

Irene jumped up and turned around. She was wearing kneepads, strapped overtop of what could only be described as high-waisted "mom" jeans. On her hands were big, yellow rubber gloves. Her hair was gathered in a pony tail that protruded from the back of a Yankees cap. Her sleeves were rolled up, and her face was pink from exertion. In her right hand, Irene held a big, stiff-bristled scrub brush, and in her left hand was a large, green, soapy sponge. "Oh dear, you shouldn't sneak up on people like that, Molly. I'm giving the floor a good cleaning."

Molly's mouth dropped open. "Don't we have a cleaning service?" she asked.

"Well, yes," Irene answered, "but every so often the linoleum needs a little TLC to keep it bright and shiny. That's where I come in."

The incredulous Molly looked at the smiling Irene in her ridiculous outfit. The only thing that Molly could think of that was worse than spending a day off with Pastor Bob was spending a day off scrubbing the church floor. What was up with that?

Molly got out her camera. "Mrs. Mitchell, can I take your picture?"

Much to Irene's dismay, Molly began to click away, taking in every detail of her kneepads, bristle brush, rubber gloves, and pink face. "Thank you," Molly said, and left Irene to her scrubbing.

Molly continued to explore. She heard the sound of children's voices and went downstairs to the day care. There, amid all that happy chatter and busy play, Molly saw one of the teachers, Mr. Rosen, sitting in the rocking chair, holding a little boy who was crying inconsolably. Tears squeezed from the little boy's closed eyes, rolled down his chubby cheeks, and left a growing wet spot on Mr. Rosen's chamois shirt. Mr. Rosen wasn't trying to fix anything. He wasn't scolding. He wasn't telling the little boy not to cry. He just rocked and let the tears fall. Molly remembered when she had been a little one in the day care, and Mr. Rosen had helped to make her feel safe and welcome. She gave Mr. Rosen a little wave, and then she took his picture.

Back upstairs, Molly tiptoed down the hall and peered around the corner into the pastor's study. There was Pastor Bob, reading and making notes, his open books cluttering the desk and floor. Bob was chewing on a pen, and it had left a large, unfortunate ink stain at the corner of his mouth. "What a loser!" Molly thought as she rolled her eyes. What Molly found most intriguing, though, was that Pastor Bob clearly loved what he was doing, reading those big, old, boring books like he was savoring every word. She could see that his computer was on, and there on the screen was writing in some strange, foreign alphabet. Molly threw open the door and took a quick picture.

"Molly! You shouldn't sneak up on people like that."

Molly demanded, pointing at the computer screen, "What's that?"

"Ah, that is the Greek New Testament, my friend. Here are the words that the risen Christ said to his disciples when he surprised them on Easter evening: '*Eiræne humin*, peace be with you.'"

"That's what Jesus sounded like?"

"Well, he may have spoken Aramaic, or even Hebrew. '*Shalom chevarim!*'" Pastor Bob said, trying out a little Hebrew for Molly's benefit. Molly nodded and switched on her tape recorder. She made Pastor Bob say it all over again. Then she wanted to know what was for lunch; it *was* getting late. With a sigh, Pastor Bob closed his precious books and put on his coat. Molly didn't tell Bob about the ink stain at the corner of his mouth that was now oozing down his chin.

They walked down the block and around the corner toward downtown and stopped in front of a dilapidated storefront that looked like it had seen better days. A handmade sign in the window said Good News Café. It was the local soup kitchen. "After you," Pastor Bob said, holding the door open for Molly.

"Pastor Bob, you can't be serious. You want me to eat here? This is for poor people."

"Is it, Molly?" Pastor Bob answered. "That must be why Jesus likes it so much."

Molly rolled her eyes and went in. Irene's husband Tubby Mitchell, who sang in the church choir, was standing behind the lunch counter. He volunteered there most week days at lunchtime. He greeted Pastor Bob with a firm handshake and heaped their plates with hot food.

While Pastor Bob visited with Tubby, Molly wandered off to find a seat at a long table. At the other end of the table were Scratch and Juice, lunchtime regulars at the Good News Café. Molly knew Scratch from the Rontaks QuikMart, where he used a corner booth like an office, waiting for day jobs and scratching lottery tickets. As a child, Juice had been christened Bruce, but in high school, his classmates had taken to calling him Bruce the Juice—and then just Juice—for his skating speed on the short track. The man was fast. Later, after he came back from the Middle East with PTSD, they called him Juice for other reasons.

Molly, still mad that Pastor Bob had brought her to the Good News Café, took it out on her pork cutlet, stabbing it repeatedly and cutting it up into about a hundred pieces. Molly noticed that Juice still had a big pile of peas on his plate, and he was looking at them like he was in love with them. "Hey, you," Molly called to Juice, "why don't you eat those peas, already?"

In response, Juice gave a sad smile and looked down at his hands. As Molly's eyes followed Juice's eyes, she could see that his hands trembled as if they had a mind of their own.

A few minutes later, Tubby Mitchell came over to the table. He sat down right next to Juice and said, "Hey, Bruce." As Molly watched, Tubby scooped the peas from Juice's plate into a coffee mug. Then, Tubby's strong hands wrapped Juice's shaky hands around the cup. While Molly watched in amazement, Juice tipped some peas into his mouth as the two men visited, chatting about the weather, and if the fish were biting, and just what kind of season the Yankees would have this year.

Molly opened her notebook and began writing furiously. After a while, she scooted down to their end of the table and asked to take their picture. Juice smiled, Tubby smiled, and Scratch made rabbit ears behind Tubby's head.

Later when Pastor Bob strolled over, he found Molly deep in conversation with her new friends. "Are you enjoying your lunch, Molly?"

"Yes, I am," Molly announced. "Pastor Bob, I have completed my research." Molly gathered up her notebook, camera, and tape recorder to leave. "I'll report to you, Pastor Bob, when I have analyzed my data. By the way, you have ink all over your face, and you look like a zombie." Molly left while everyone laughed, and Tubby Mitchell tried to help Pastor Bob wipe the ink stain off his chin.

The next Sunday morning before the service, while Pastor Bob made some last-minute additions to the prayers of the people, Molly knocked on his office door. "C'mon in!" he called out.

Molly pushed the door open and stood in front of his desk. In her hands she clutched a wrinkly piece of paper. "Here," she said, holding it out to Pastor Bob. "This is a summary of my findings."

Pastor Bob saw that Molly had written a poem or psalm of sorts. He took the paper and smoothed it out on his desktop. He could see that she had worked hard, erasing and crossing out words until she had it just right. Pastor Bob looked from the paper to Molly.

She rolled her eyes. "Read it, Pastor Bob!"
He did. This is what Molly had written.

"I saw him, the risen Lord.

When the bread broke

and the silent spoke,

I felt him near.

On hands and knees,

he does the work

of a servant

with secret joy.

With strong arms

and tender heart,

he welcomes children,

holds their tears.

He feasts

upon the Word

and speaks peace

in many tongues.

He feeds the hungry,

the hopeless,

the down and out,

without judgment.

He is the rock

that steadies

the least of these.

I saw him, the risen Lord."

When Pastor Bob looked up from Molly's poem, she could see that he had tears in his eyes. "Pastor Bob," Molly said, "I'm sorry I called you a zombie."

Pastor Bob laughed, "Believe me, Molly. I've been called much worse. Apology accepted."

"Christ is risen!" Molly celebrated.

Pastor Bob celebrated right back, "He is risen, indeed! Alleluia!"

6

Generous to All

"For there is no distinction between Jew and Greek; the same Lord
is Lord of all and is generous to all who call on him."

—Romans 10:12

It was a lovely, late summer evening. Goldenrod waved from the roadside. A first, few red leaves tinged the maples. The sun, low above the lake, pulsed orange in the rearview mirror. Pastor Bob and Marge drove with windows down. Jimmy Buffet, playing on the radio, invited them to Margaritaville. Bob was thinking how nice it was that they'd had enough cool evenings to tame the mosquitoes when Marge asked, "So, what do you think it's about this time?"

Bob considered feigning ignorance, but he knew that wouldn't work with Marge. Instead, he sighed, "The Lord only knows, but you have to admit that it's an awfully nice invitation."

Marge responded with a knowing look and a grin, "Oh, I'm sure they're cooking up something real good for you."

They drove on in silence while Bob tried to ignore the fluttering feeling that he got in his gut when trouble was brewing. Now that he thought about it, pretty much every time Tommy and Kitten Stewart had asked him out to their impressive camp on the big lake there had been a hidden agenda. It had started Bob's first year at the Presbyterian Church. The young pastor had been thrilled to be invited to their nineteenth-century lodge with its hand-hewn beams and massive stone fireplace. The view from their living room was one of the most spectacular in the North Country, and Kitten's cooking was equally legendary. Village wags had it that Tommy's family had made a fortune in logging and then multiplied it by running liquor down from Montreal during Prohibition, but Bob had a hard time reconciling that gossip with the distinguished man in crisply pressed khakis who greeted him with a firm handshake. "Bob," Tommy thundered, "We've been meaning to have you over for a little chat for months now."

On his first visit, the "little chat" had been about Ulee McVicker, who admittedly was a tough man to love, especially in the winter months. Ulee was one of those old-timers who foreswore bathing from the time the ice went in until it went out. Pastor Bob was fairly confident that beneath his worn, woolen, Sunday go-to-church apparel, Ulee wore a red union suit— with a trap door. By about mid-March, folks gave Ulee a wide berth where he sat in the back pew. Tommy and Kitten seemed to think that Pastor Bob should assert his spiritual authority by persuading Ulee that cleanliness was next to godliness, all year round.

Over the years, there had been other little chats. When Liz Williams, the local cardiologist, had to spend some time in rehab, Tommy and Kitten had suggested that Bob counsel her to make a fresh start at another hospital, maybe down in the capital region, far from local scandal. When Ross Smith and David Jaworski bought the big bed and breakfast on the hill and joined the church, Tommy and Kitten expressed their genuine concern about what welcoming a same-sex couple might mean. There had even been a brief spell after the worship committee had invested in a new electronic piano when Tommy and Kitten had boycotted Sunday mornings until Bob convinced them that it was not the first step in launching a praise band.

It wasn't that Tommy and Kitten were mean-spirited. In fact, Bob and others at the church really liked them. They loved the Lord and were kind, unfailingly generous, and plenty of fun to be around. But they had some particular notions about how to run a church. The fact that Tommy's ancestors had been among the church's founding members might have had something to do with their sense of proprietary righteousness. Someone had to ensure that things were done decently and in order. At the Presbyterian Church, that job fell to Tommy and Kitten.

As always, the dinner that night was fabulous—thick steaks cooked on the grill, buttery twice-baked potatoes, a big salad topped with toasted nuts and fragrant crumbles of goat cheese, and crème brulee for dessert. Bob was just beginning to think that he had been uncharitable in suspecting an ulterior motive for the visit when Kitten stood up, looking the picture of perfection with her manicured nails and classic up-do. "Well," Kitten purred, "why don't Marge and I do a little clearing while you two get some fresh air on the deck." Marge shot Bob an I-told-you-so look as she cleared his plate and the two men walked out into the evening.

The moon was up, its reflection rippling across the lake. The loons were putting on quite a show, their tremolo calls echoing in the dark. Drawn in by the night's spell, Bob almost forgot where he was and what was afoot. Tommy didn't, and it didn't take him long to get to the point. "Bob, have you given any thought to a dress code for your elders? Maybe not every Sunday, but certainly on first Sundays when they serve the Lord's Supper." Although Bob's blank expression suggested that dress codes were about as far from his mind as the identity of Justin Bieber's latest girlfriend, Tommy plowed on. "You know, Bob, two Sunday's ago I was served by an elder wearing flip flops, shorts, and a Hawaiian shirt. I can assure you that I am not the only person in the pews who feels that we need some standards about these things."

When Bob saw how utterly sincere Tommy seemed to be, he squelched the urge to remind him that Jesus wore sandals, too. Instead, Bob said, "I assume you are talking about Chris." Chris Nelson was by far the youngest elder on the session. When Chris was elected, Bob knew that the young man would push some folks out of their comfort zones. Chris had a shaved head and a scraggly goatee. Both ears were pierced, and tattooed bracelets encircled both wrists. From late spring until early fall, Chris could be spotted around the village in cargo shorts, sandals, and a seemingly endless selection of loud, colorful Hawaiian shirts. Although Chris's appearance could be off-putting, Bob had found the young man to be an excellent elder—energetic, creative, hardworking, and excited about living for Jesus.

"Well, Tommy," Bob responded, "We're not getting any younger. Has it occurred to you that part of welcoming a new generation into church leadership will demand that we accept them as they are, even with their, uh, different sense of style? Don't you think God can work in new ways through new people?"

The shocked look on Tommy's face said that neither Tommy nor Kitten could possibly imagine such a thing. "I tell you what," Bob continued, "I'll let the session know how you feel. Would you and Kitten like to come to the next meeting and let your concerns be known?"

This was clearly not the answer that Tommy had anticipated. Looking disappointed, Tommy said, "I think I've already made myself clear, Bob."

As Bob and Marge drove back to town, they decided that it would probably be a while before their next dinner invitation from the Stewarts.

Suddenly, Bob felt rather weary. He wondered if the apostle Paul had felt this way when he tried to convince his Jewish critics that Gentiles truly were welcome to the covenant, that God's love was limitless and generous to all. He sighed and Marge reached over to give his knee a reassuring pat. "Cheer up, honey," she smiled. "Cold weather will be here soon enough, and Chris Nelson will be forced to trade his shorts and sandals for Carhartts and boots. And those Hawaiian shirts? They'll be hidden beneath bulky, wool sweaters."

It would be months before Bob got a call from Tommy or Kitten. They were friendly enough on Sunday mornings, but there was a strained quality to their smiles that let Bob know that he had disappointed them. Then one afternoon as he returned from lunch, Linda, Bob's secretary, handed him a phone message from Kitten, saying to call her immediately on her cell phone. Bob dialed the number and listened while Kitten explained that Tommy had a heart attack while shoveling snow. He was going to make it, but he needed bypass surgery. Would Bob come to the hospital, and add them to the prayer list? The brittle edge to Kitten's voice told Bob that her need for a pastor had overcome the anger and disappointment she had harbored. Bob asked Linda to notify the prayer chain, and then he drove to the hospital, saying his own prayers along the way.

When Bob walked into Tommy's hospital room, he met the cardiologist, Liz Williams, on her way out. It was a good thing for Tommy and Kitten that Liz hadn't relocated to the capital region to avoid the local scandal of her time in rehab. According to the thankful Kitten, Liz had saved Tommy's life. Liz had seen he was in trouble from the minute she was called to the ER. She had given him aspirin and provided just the right treatment to minimize damage to the heart. Liz then referred them to the best heart surgeon in the North Country for Tommy's bypass.

Weeks later, Bob realized that Tommy's heart attack had given both Tommy and Kitten a change of heart. One snowy afternoon, Bob and Marge drove out to the Stewart camp with a loaf of homemade bread and a pot of Marge's chicken noodle soup. As they pulled into the driveway, Chris Nelson, wearing a fluorescent green, down jacket, was backing the snowblower into the garage, having just finished clearing the walkways. Chris had earbuds in and was clearly grooving to some music that no one else could hear. The young man waved hello before grabbing a snow shovel and walking around back to clear the deck. As they waited for Kitten to answer the door, Marge whispered, "Do you think he's got a Hawaiian shirt on under that jacket?"

Kitten ushered them into the great room with its spectacular view. A fire burned in the massive stone fireplace. Tommy was kicked back in his recliner, looking a little worn out but clearly on the mend. As they visited, they could see Chris Nelson, wielding his shovel on the deck, where months before Bob had appreciated the cry of the loons. Before long, Chris had worked up a sweat. He stripped off the down jacket and Bob was now certain that he could see the hem of a Hawaiian shirt poking out from beneath Chris's wool sweater. Bob, Marge, Kitten, and Tommy talked about the snow and cardiac rehab and heart-healthy diets. After a while, they lapsed into a comfortable silence, watching the fire.

Tommy began, gesturing to the stack of firewood on the hearth, "You know, Bob, I can't begin to tell you how good folks have been to us. Do you see that wood? Ulee McVicker has been out just about every other day to chop and haul wood for Kitten." Kitten nodded brightly, clearly no longer troubled by Ulee's winter funk.

She continued, "And you won't believe what Ross Smith and David Jaworski did. On our first night home after the surgery, they showed up with flowers and a catered dinner. Boy, were we blessed! Those people can sure plan a party." Bob wasn't sure what to say in response to that.

Fortunately, they were all distracted by Chris, who was now making a life-sized snowman out back. Chris stuck long twigs all over the top of its head, as if it had some sort of crazy, electric afro. He stepped back and surveyed his work, and then he gave it a finishing touch —two large breasts. Kitten gasped, but everyone else roared with laughter.

They threw another log on the fire and chatted about this and that until Tommy started to look tired. Kitten and Marge withdrew to the kitchen to compare chicken-soup recipes while Bob prayed with Tommy. After the "Amen," Tommy shook Bob's hand. "You know, Bob, I'm beginning to think you are right about welcoming people, accepting them as they are. Maybe God does do new things in new ways every now and then. Just don't expect me to be wearing Hawaiian shirts and flip flops to church anytime soon."

Bob looked out at the big-breasted snowwoman and gave his old friend a pat on the back, saying, "That's alright, Tommy. I don't think Jesus will object to what you wear one bit."

7

Divided

"Do you think I have come to bring peace to the earth? No, I tell you, but rather division! From now on, five in one household will be divided: three against two and two against three."

—LUKE 12:51

"We have been called to heal wounds, to unite what has fallen apart, and to bring home those who have lost their way."

—SAINT FRANCIS OF ASSISI

Pastor Bob should have known there would be trouble when Pica Bernard insisted on baptizing the baby. Her husband Peter was in northern Quebec, leading a group on one of those high-priced, fly-in fishing trips. A prosperous entrepreneur, Peter was often on the road. Some said he was the richest man in town, and his flamboyant personality matched the size of his bank account. From his Main Street storefront, Peter sold sporting goods, rods, and guns, but excursions were his bread and butter. Despite the fact that the baby was coming soon, Peter had scheduled not one trip but four, back to back. Prestigious clients from the city and as far afield as California were signed on to follow Peter into the backcountry on a quest for salmon, moose, or bear. When asked when he would be home, the man was cagey.

It was a bold act of independence. Pica gave her child the name John—after John the Baptist. Pica was pious, or at least as pious as a Presbyterian could be. On the Sunday morning of the baptism, Pica told Pastor Bob that she hoped that her little one, like his namesake, might one day be a pastor—a good one, too, with Pica's heart for prayer and Peter's gifts for leadership and

34

adventure. The thought of anyone who could reconcile the spirits of the pious Pica and the bombastic Peter was enough to put a smile on Bob's face.

Of course, when Peter eventually returned home, the baby got a name change. John was relegated to a middle name, and Peter dubbed the boy Francis, after French Canada, which had been so good for Peter's bank account—but everyone called the boy Franco. Though Pica hoped that her child would be a man of the cloth, Peter simply hoped that his son would sell a lot of cloth—Gore-Tex parkas, hip waders, down jackets and vests, wool shirts and pants. Pica never forgot her child's first name, and neither did Pastor Bob.

When Franco was a boy, his father brought him along on trips, took him to the store downtown, and taught him all about the business. When he was still just a youngster, Franco knew how to welcome customers, show off the parkas and long johns to their best advantage, and even strike a promising deal. On Franco's sixteenth birthday, Peter, already planning to entrust his business to his son, gave the boy a key to the store and had a nice sign painted for the front window. It read, "Adventure Unlimited – Bernard & Son." While Peter took clients ever farther afield to fish the Yukon or hunt bighorn sheep in the Canadian Rockies, Franco helped Pica run the store. When Peter returned to town, filled with wild tales of adventure, he bore gifts: a necklace carved from walrus ivory for Pica; a pup with enormous paws that looked more wolf than malamute for Franco.

Peter's plans for a father-son business empire might have unfolded seamlessly if it hadn't been for Scratch Johnson's brush with homelessness. One summer afternoon, as Franco bargained with a customer over the sale of a custom fly rod, Scratch wandered down Main Street. He had fallen off the wagon—badly. He had the shakes. His clothes hung loose on his scare-crow frame. He stood in the doorway to the shop and cast an apprising eye upon Franco. "Hey, son, how about a little help here? I'm not looking for a handout. Give me a broom and I'll sweep your walk."

Franco paused. He looked from his homeless neighbor to his prosper-ous customer—the two people could not have been more different. Franco's brow creased in wonder and concern at the incongruity of the human condi-tion. Before the boy could fetch the broom out of the back room, Scratch caught a whiff of lunch from the Good News Café and ambled away.

What happened next caused the trouble. Franco struck a deal and hustled his customer—with a newly purchased fly rod, some hand-tied flies, and a fly-fishing vest—out the door. Then, Franco tucked money from the sale into his pocket and ran out of the shop and down the street, away from his father's sporting-goods empire.

Franco caught up with Scratch at the Good News Café, where he had already filled his tray in the buffet line and taken a seat at a corner table, shoveling forkfuls of tuna-noodle casserole and green beans into his mouth. Franco took a seat at the table, caught his breath, and turned his pockets out. Three crisp, hundred-dollar bills lay on the table between the teenager and the homeless man. "Look, mister," Franco said, "I think you could use this more than me."

Scratch choked on his lunch. He and the boy spent the next hour talking about their very different lives. At the end of the conversation, Scratch stood up. He pushed two of the hundred-dollar bills back across the table to Franco. "I'll just drink that, son, but this," he said, tucking the last bill into a very worn-looking wallet, "this is a bus ticket to my sister's. Maybe she'll help get me into rehab." Franco wasn't sure what rehab was, but he hoped the money would be useful.

When Peter returned home from Canada and folks told him of Franco's crazy business dealings, the father wasn't pleased. Red-faced at the dinner table, he lectured his son: "Francis John Bernard, I thought I could trust you. What kind of businessman are you, giving away the store? C'mon, boy, straighten up."

But for Franco, nothing was the same. Everywhere, he saw a world of need—neighbors waiting in line at the food pantry, mentally ill adults smoking on street corners near halfway houses, dogs living on chains outside rusty trailers—that he had never before imagined. He felt a terrible tension within himself, caught between his desire to make his father happy and his longing to do something that would make a difference in that hidden world of suffering. When Pastor Bob got wind of Franco's unrest, he suggested that the boy try his hand at community service.

Franco took to volunteering after school at Sunny Vue. He would take his guitar and Wolfie, who had long since grown into his enormous paws, and visit the residents. He played a little music and told stories about the beauty of nature and the wilds of French Canada while Wolfie did tricks for biscuits. It was a good thing to do, but the tension within Franco wound tighter. In the middle of the night, he would awaken with a sense that the answer to his questions hovered just beyond the reach of his young imagination.

One evening, Franco thought he had found his purpose. It was his senior year of high school. Pica had been leaving college brochures out on the kitchen table, and when Peter was in town, he mused aloud about how great it would be to soon have Franco full-time in the store or running trips. Then, late one night, while Franco and friends Todd Mitchell and Bruce MacLeod were watching *Saturday Night Live* on the basement television, they saw it—a Marine Corps ad. A striking young woman in an impeccable uniform brandished a saber. Men in helicopters soared above foreign landscapes. Waves crashed on unknown shores. Small children laughed and clambered for the attention of smiling, young soldiers. Music, both noble and evocative, played. The three young men watched transfixed, all coming to the simultaneous conclusion that they needed to enlist.

It didn't go well for any of them. Todd was killed by an improvised explosive device, midway through their first deployment in Iraq. Bruce did four tours, but he never recovered from seeing his friend blown to bits. They said he had PTSD. After the Second Battle of Fallujah, Franco was abducted by Baath separatists and spent the better part of a year as a hostage.

When Franco was freed, he was welcomed home as a hero with a parade down Main Street. The high school band played "Stars and Stripes Forever," the twirlers tried out a new routine with flaming batons, and Franco rode with Wolfie in the back of a Cadillac convertible with the top down. Even though Franco's only experience of having a beard was during his captivity, the Brothers of the Bush, men of all ages with flowing beards, carried signs that said, "Welcome Home, Franco!" and "You're our Hero!" and "Even Iraq is better with a beard!"

The *Little City News* did a story. When the reporter asked Franco what he remembered most about his captors, he thought a long time. Finally, he sighed and said, "I remember that they were very poor, but they always gave me food. I remember that, underneath it all, they seemed just as frightened as I was. I remember that we tried to hate each other, but in the end we couldn't." He suspected that his escape was the result of intentional negligence by a Baath soldier of about the same age, his cell left unlocked one night after dinner. When folks read that, they thought Franco must have Stockholm syndrome. The captive had found an alarming compassion for his captors.

Franco was invited to Washington, D.C. He met the president, received a medal, shook hands with his personal hero, Senator John McCain, and toured the Capitol. But it wasn't the people and places of power, or even the National Air and Space Museum, that made the biggest impression upon Franco. It was the homeless, sleeping on subway grates a block from the White House. He saw disabled vets, junkies, and old people pushing shopping carts filled with rubbish, all looking like they could benefit from a few meals at the Good News Café.

On Sunday morning, as Franco was coming out of the New York Avenue Presbyterian Church, he fell over a homeless woman sleeping in the side doorway. When Franco looked closely, he saw that, although she couldn't have been much more than fourteen or so, she was pregnant. She must have been very tired because she didn't wake up. Franco sat down on the doorstep of the church and wept. He picked up the little begging bowl that she had put out, just in case anyone felt charitable after church, and he solicited donations on her behalf. When the basket was full, he hid it safely under her blanket and left, imagining her surprise when she awakened and learned that she would eat that day and the next.

Franco went home and back to his father's shop. His old sense of inner tension and turmoil only grew more intense. At Pica's urging, Franco talked to Pastor Bob about it, this feeling that he was supposed to be doing something significant with his life. Franco told Bob how sad he felt. He seemed to be hurting his father's feelings, disappointing his mother, and even failing his country. Bob listened and prayed. "Franco," he said, "I don't know what the Lord has in store for you, but I do trust that, if you listen, there will be an answer."

Then, one day there was. As Franco prayed in the church sanctuary, Jesus spoke to him. In fact, Jesus stepped right out of the dusty old picture by the side door, the one that showed him walking on the water. Jesus stretched and walked across the sanctuary floor until he stood right in front of Franco. "Franco, my brother! I've got a job for you. Go and repair my house which is falling into ruins." Then Jesus turned around and got back into the picture. If Jesus hadn't left behind a big splotch on the carpet, where his robe, wet from all those years of walking on the water, had rested on the rug, Franco would not have believed it. Franco had never seen himself as a general contractor, or even the church sexton for that matter, but now he knew what he needed to do: serve God by fixing up churches.

That Monday morning, Franco went to his father's store, and he put into practice everything that his father had ever told him about being a good businessman. He welcomed customers and suggested merchandise. He struck amazing deals that left his customers happy and filled Peter's cash register to overflowing. The father rejoiced, thinking that at last Franco had gotten a little common sense and decided to really join him in the business.

But when payday arrived, Franco cashed his check and went to the hardware store. He bought a lawn mower, house paint and brushes, shingles, nails, an extension ladder, and lots of Windex. Then, Franco went down to the little church on Pliny Mill Road, the one that had sat empty for several years. He cut the grass and scraped and painted the walls. He fixed the roof and cleaned all the windows. His church-improvement project took up all his time off for weeks. Surveying his finished work, Franco felt satisfied. He was headed in the right direction.

When Peter heard what Francis was doing with his time away from the business, he was angry. He wasn't paying his son good money only to have him throw it away on some crazy church-improvement project. Didn't Franco see that he was born to be a businessman and not some religious handyman? This was absolutely not in the best interest of the family or the business.

Peter tried to change his son's mind. "Franco, you're breaking my heart here! How can you do this to us? Haven't I given you everything? Don't you love me?" But no amount of arguing, threats, or even blows would sway Franco.

Finally, Peter did the unimaginable—he appealed to the church. If Franco wouldn't listen to his family, then maybe he would have ears to hear Pastor Bob. One evening, Peter, Pica, and Franco sat on the couch in the pastor's study. Bob noticed how upset the father was, bristling with frustration and anger. He saw how happy the son was to be doing something that felt to him like he was serving God. He also noticed that Franco had a black eye, and he suspected that he knew where that had come from. Pica was silent and withdrawn. While Peter pled his case, Bob listened carefully. He saw that, with every word of the father's aggrieved story, Franco seemed to grow smaller until he looked like a little boy again— slumped on the couch and kicking at a wrinkle in the carpet—staring up at the picture of John the Baptist hanging on the wall.

When Peter was finished, Pastor Bob thought about the day that he had baptized Franco—that moment of promise and possibility—with the mother's hope of a spiritual calling still in his ears. "Well, well, Francis John, what do you think about all this? I want to hear from you. What do you have to say to your father?"

There was a gentleness in Bob's voice that gave Franco the courage to speak. He sat up straight and slowly shook his head. "Dad, I can't be the son you want me to be. I can't be a businessman. Jesus has other work for me to do. He wants me to repair his church."

Then, just in case Peter hadn't understood the utter seriousness of his words, Franco stood up and stripped off everything that he was wearing: his North Face jacket and soft fleece vest, his flannel shirt and sturdy Carhartt work pants, the Vasque boots and Smartwool socks—even his boxer shorts. All the beautiful merchandise that had come from his father's store lay in a pile on the floor of the pastor's study. Franco stood there naked as the day he was born when Pica named him John and dreamed about her baby becoming a great church leader. When the last stitch of clothing hit the floor, Franco thought that he had never felt so light, or happy, or free.

Pastor Bob broke the awkward silence that followed, saying, "Peter, I know that you have your heart set on Franco following in your footsteps, but it sounds like the Lord has other plans for him. Can't you find it within your heart to bless him? Let's pray about it." They prayed together—the naked Francis, the enraged Peter, and the silent Pica. When Bob finished, Peter stood up and left. The next morning, he took a can of black spray paint and obliterated the "& Son" from the sign in front of the store. They say he never spoke to Franco again.

Franco also disappointed his mother's hope that he would become a pastor in any conventional sense of the word. About three months after the failed attempt at family reconciliation, Franco came to see Bob with a bold plan. He wanted to use the old church on Pliny Mill Road as a shelter, where the homeless could find respite and support to get back on their feet. Bob and Franco took their plans to the presbytery, which agreed to a five-year trial run. Funding for Franco's big dream, the On Belay Community, fell into place. Folks liked Franco, and he had many affluent contacts from his years at the store. When he talked to them of the power of love and the beauty of nature to help and heal, they got caught up in his enthusiasm and broke out their checkbooks. Before long, Franco, who had lost a father, found that he had a strange new sort of family that the Lord had given him to love. The inner tension, which had troubled him for so long, was finally gone.

In the years to come, Pastor Bob would sometimes stop in front of that picture of Jesus walking on the water and ask the Lord what he could have done to reconcile father and son. It felt as if the prince of peace had brought the sword of division to at least one family in the village. In time, Bob accepted that following the Lord sometimes takes young people in unexpected directions, and that can be hard for parents. He just hoped he wouldn't have to go through that with his own son, Paul.

8

Something to Sing About

"My soul magnifies the Lord, and my Spirit rejoices in God my Savior."

—LUKE 1:46B-47

Lenore Claiborne stood behind the counter of The Rustic Gourmet, her shop that sold cookware, linens, coffees, and mixes for savory and sweet treats. This was Lenore's busiest Christmas season ever. All day she ran between assisting customers and ringing up sales. Over at the wrapping table, her teenage helper, Molly Hall, was hidden by a tower of mixing bowls, mugs, dish cloths, and scone mixes, all ready for holiday paper and festive bows. While Lenore helped the last shoppers of the day, the shop cat, Jacques Pepin, threaded around her ankles, meowing plaintively that it was past dinner time.

At 6:45 p.m., Lenore locked the door and shuddered as she surveyed the shop. The kitchen linens, so neatly folded that morning, were heaped in a shapeless pile. Coffee beans littered the self-service counter. Curls of ribbon and scraps of paper had piled up beneath the wrapping table at Molly's feet. Lenore fed Jacques Pepin, who was now yowling with outrage at the lateness of his supper. She ate the remaining snack samples and chased them down with a generous glass of eggnog. So much to do, so little time. When Molly Hall spoke up behind her, Lenore almost jumped out of her skin. "You head over to choir practice, Mrs. Claiborne. I'll clean up here."

The Christmas cantata was always a highlight of Lenore's holiday season. This year, Lenore was singing the Magnificat. All December long, Lenore had practiced the bright notes of Mary's Song, so sweet and prophetic. As Lenore walked over to the church, thoughts of the Magnificat were eclipsed by the long list of things she needed to do before Christmas.

The drumming of her boots on the snowy sidewalk began to sound like a muster call to battle. In addition to her work at The Rustic Gourmet, she had holiday baking to do, the tree to decorate, guest bedrooms to prepare, bathrooms to clean, and last-minute gifts to purchase. There was goulash to make, too—Lenore usually made Pastor Bob a Crock-Pot of her famous recipe so that he, Marge, and Paul could eat at church between Christmas Eve services.

By the time Lenore reached the church, beads of perspiration dotted her upper lip. The chancel was crowded. Frank Duncan, the choir director, had recruited volunteers to play violin, cello, trumpet, and flute. Frank smiled a welcome at Lenore. "Perfect timing, Lenore. How about if we run through your solo?"

Lenore rose as the piano, violin, and flute began their evocative introduction. At just the right moment, she breathed deep and opened her mouth to sing. But Lenore's voice sounded nothing like the bright, sweet, prophetic song of Mary. Instead, Lenore sounded a lot like the plaintive cries of the cat Jacques Pepin, pining for his supper. "My soul, it magnifies the Lord . . ." Lenore's mouth snapped shut.

Frank Duncan looked up, his hands poised above the keyboard. In Lenore's overactive imagination, every choir member turned to look at her in horror, all the strings broke on the violin, and the mute popped out of the trumpet's bell in protest. She struggled through her solo and left as soon as the last note of the last carol was sung.

At home, Lenore found husband Steve asleep in front of the television, looking worn and thin. This was a busy time of year for him, too. Steve wasn't much of a cook, but at her place at the kitchen table waited a green salad and a generous glass of wine. In the oven was a casserole of macaroni and cheese. Lenore drank the wine, ate all the mac and cheese, and ignored the salad. After dinner, she put on her apron and began her Christmas baking. Roused by the smell of Lenore's good cooking, Steve came in to say goodnight. He helped himself to a peanut butter thumbprint, gave Lenore a kiss, and said, "Don't you worry about the dishes, sweetheart. I'll tackle them in the morning."

The next day, Lenore got to the shop extra early, where Jacques Pepin's breakfast yowls reminded her of her solo at choir practice the night before. She fed Jacques, bagged up the gifts that Molly had neatly wrapped, prepared fresh snacks, and lit her favorite cranberry-spice Christmas candle. Lenore was feeling a bit more like her old self until she unlocked the shop door and welcomed her first customer of the day—Pastor Bob.

Some people get sad and teary when under stress, but Lenore, she got crabby. Just seeing Bob, Lenore's imagination took to new flights of fancy. She imagined Frank Duncan calling Pastor Bob in the pre-dawn hours to lament about her poor vocal performance. She imagined Bob there in her shop on a special mission to charm her back into the dulcet tones of Mary's song. Before Bob could even extend a friendly greeting, she unleashed upon him a tirade about long hours to work, a house to clean, baking to finish, and last-minute gifts to buy. And who did Bob think he was, anyway, to talk to her about how she sang Mary's song?

Now, Pastor Bob was no stranger to Lenore Claiborne's tongue lashings, but she had really outdone herself this time. When Lenore paused to catch her breath, Bob reached out a hand to pat her generous shoulder reassuringly and share his sympathy. "I hear you, Lenore. This time of year is absolutely overwhelming. Believe me, I know. Look, I just came in to pick up a Christmas gift for Marge. She's asking for an Ove Glove, and I have no idea what that is. Can you help me?"

As Lenore helped Bob shop, she felt a little sheepish about her tirade, but she wasn't about to apologize. And if he asked to pray with her, she was going to kick him out.

As he left the shop, Bob turned back with a serious look and said, "Lenore, have you thought about Mary?" Before Lenore could unleash a fresh tirade, Bob hurried on, "Mary was young, unwed, pregnant. She lived in an occupied country, in poverty we can't even begin to imagine. But she rejoiced amid all that trouble. She knew she was blessed and God would bless the world through her child. She decided that she had something to sing about."

Lenore debated throwing a bright red, KitchenAid mixer at Bob. Instead, she said, "Gee, thanks a lot, Bob." As the door jingled shut, Lenore decided that she was crossing Bob's Christmas Eve goulash off her to-do list.

The day before Christmas dawned with a festive, powdery coating of fresh snow. When Lenore rose, she saw that Steve had been up and busy. The bathrooms were sparkling clean, and a sensible bowl of oatmeal and glass of juice awaited her on the kitchen table. As Steve pulled on his overcoat and gave her a goodbye kiss, he said, "Now, don't worry about the guest rooms, Lenore. Amy is arriving early and has offered to get the beds made up for us. The kids will do the tree. I've got to work late, but I'll see you at church for the Christmas cantata. Bye."

Lenore was eating her oatmeal and thinking black thoughts about singing the Magnificat when the doorbell rang. It was Pastor Bob's wife Marge, looking annoyingly perky and holding a Crock-Pot.

"Hey, Lenore," Marge said while handing her the slow cooker. "We know you usually do this for us, but this year we wanted to do this for you." From the Crock-Pot, there arose the tempting aroma of North Country goulash, which she was sure wouldn't be as good as her own, but it was a thoughtful gesture.

When Lenore arrived at the shop, Molly was already there. "I'm off from school today, Mrs. Claiborne, so I thought I'd come in a little early."

Jacques Pepin the cat had been fed and was washing his whiskers with a satisfied look. The sweet and savory samples were out. Even the cranberry-spice Christmas candle was lit. The shopping day passed in a swirl of shoppers shopping, register ringing, and Molly wrapping. When they locked the door behind the last customer at five o'clock, Molly took charge. "You go home and get some dinner, Mrs. Claiborne. Jacques and I will close up. I'll see you at church tonight." For a moment, the prospect of singing the Magnificat filled Lenore with terrified anticipation, but she gave Molly a hug of thanksgiving and rushed off to Hank Tinker's Outdoor Emporium to buy a final gift for Steve.

That night, Lenore sat on the chancel feeling weary and defeated. The pleats on her choir robe strained over her ample bosom, reminding her that she needed to go back to Weight Watchers in the new year. Her voice had not improved. During practice, the harsh, shrill tones of Jacques Pepin the cat continued to haunt her vocal cords. She had hit all the notes, but it hadn't been pretty. Lenore thought reluctantly about what Pastor Bob had said about Mary. Despite it all, Mary had found something to sing about.

Lenore gave a little wave to Steve and her family when they arrived early to claim their favorite pew alongside Maybelle Howard. She noticed Molly Hall, sitting with teenage friends in the back of the church. Pastor Bob rushed by in search of the lighter for the Advent wreath, which had mysteriously disappeared. Lenore smiled a little at her fellow choristers, many of whom she had sung with for twenty years. She suspected that all those people would still love her, whether she sounded like Mary of Nazareth or Jacques Pepin the cat. She suspected that God might still love her, despite her crabbiness and Christmas stress.

When it came time for Lenore's solo, she rose. With thanksgiving she listened to that beautiful introduction of piano, violin, and flute. With a full heart, she breathed deep and opened her mouth to sing. And out came the shrill tones of Jacques Pepin, yowling for his late dinner. But four notes into the solo, just as Lenore sang the word "magnified," her voice found its sweet spot, and the melody rang out in the silvery tones of Mary—young, pregnant, vulnerable, impoverished, but with so much to sing about.

The morning after Christmas, Lenore was back at the shop. With her Christmas stress gone, Lenore hummed a little song as she added some sardines to Jacques Pepin's kibble and scratched his ears. Midway through her morning, Pastor Bob came in with a five o'clock shadow, looking like he was making the most of his week off.

"Hey, Lenore," he greeted her, "Marge sent me in for another Ove Glove. She says just one won't do her much good." He found another glove and filled a bag with fair-trade, Sumatran, dark-roast, coffee beans.

As Lenore rang up the purchase, Bob ventured, "Great job on Christmas Eve. I can tell that you really thought about Mary, how your voice started with that stressed, fearful edge, and then broke forth with faith and strength. I think it was our best cantata ever."

Lenore bagged Bob's purchase. She debated admitting that her performance had nothing to do with her artistic expression. Instead, she handed Bob his purchase and smiled. "Well, Bob, I guess I found that I've got something to sing about after all."

9

Bread of Life

Jesus said to them, "I am the bread of life. Whoever comes to me will never be hungry, and whoever believes in me will never be thirsty."

—JOHN 6:35

Maude Beecher had been baking the communion bread for more years than most people could remember. She took over from old Bart Rockwell, who died the same year they discovered that streptomycin was a whole lot better than cold air at curing tuberculosis. Before Bart, Elvie Smith, a charter member of the church, had done the baking. They say Elvie baked the first communion loaf when the sanctuary was still under construction, without any windows and just rough wooden benches for pews. Other churches in town modernized and traded whole loaves for tiny squares of Wonder Bread or itty-bitty, germ-free, gluten-free, fat-free wafers, but the Presbyterians held on to their tradition. Someone was always baking bread on Saturday to be broken and served on Sunday. There was even a special recipe on a worn and yellowed slip of paper that had been passed from Elvie to Bart to Maude, with the title "BREAD OF LIFE" written in a fine hand across the top.

One day, as Pastor Bob was working in his study, he heard a knock and looked up to see Maude Beecher at the door in a lavender pantsuit and orthopedic shoes. She came in and took a seat. They visited about family and summer garden plans. At last, Maude got to the point. "Bob," she said, holding her hands up in front of her, "it's time for me to pass the torch. You need to find a new baker."

Bob looked at Maude's hands. Her fingers were twisted and bent with age. The skin was fine and papery, and a roadmap of ropy veins snaked across the backs. When had she gotten so old?

"How do you feel about giving up the baking?" Bob wanted to know.

Maude leaned back in her chair and shrugged, "Oh, I guess I'm ready. Bart Rockwell told me that there would come a day when I would know it was time to retire, and it just feels like this is it. I'm ready to train someone new."

"I hear you, Maude," Pastor Bob answered. "You have been a good and faithful servant. We'll see who the Lord raises up to fill those sensible shoes of yours. Let's pray about it."

Finding a replacement for Maude was not easy. First, Pastor Bob put an article in the *Tidbits*, but no one even commented about it. This made Pastor Bob wonder if anyone even read the newsletter. Next, he put an announcement in the Sunday bulletin—not a bite. Finally, Bob had to resort to personal invitations, but even these weren't fruitful. Pastor Bob had just about run out of people to ask when he saw Heather Rodriguez picking up her children from day care. She had an infant in a Snugli, a toddler by the hand, and an impatient kindergartener telling her, "Hurry up!" Pastor Bob had heard that José had gotten a big promotion at the quarry, and Heather was leaving her job to be a stay-at-home mom. Maybe Heather would be open to a new opportunity to serve the church.

But when Pastor Bob asked Heather if she would be interested in baking communion bread, she laughed. "Pastor Bob, the last time I made anything even remotely resembling a loaf of bread, it was in an Easy-Bake Oven. I wouldn't know where to begin."

Pastor Bob assured Heather that no experience was necessary—Maude Beecher would teach her everything she needed to know. Heather's resolve seemed to be softening, so Bob looked at the three little ones and did some improvising. "I'll tell you what, Heather. I'll come over on first Saturdays and help José with the kids until you're all trained."

Now, Heather could not remember the last time that she had an offer of free child care. Giddy with the thought of a few Saturday mornings off, Heather found herself saying, "Pastor Bob, looks like you've found yourself a baker."

On the first Saturdays in May, June, and July, Pastor Bob showed up bright and early at the Rodriguez house, and Heather headed over to Maude Beecher's home for baking lessons. Maude greeted Heather at the door with an old-fashioned apron tied around her generous waist. She handed a matching apron to Heather, and the two women went back to the kitchen.

An enormous earthenware bowl stood in the middle of the counter. Next to it was a large, worn, wooden spoon. All the ingredients were lined up, ready for action: unbleached flour, milk, butter, yeast, salt, an egg, and just a little bit of sugar. Heather picked up a scrap of paper, titled "BREAD OF LIFE" and yellowed with age. "Hmm. I don't know, Maude. This sounds serious. I'm not so sure it's a good idea, you training me."

Maude just smiled and patted Heather's hand, "Honey, I said the same thing when Bart Rockwell began to teach me. I couldn't boil water, but Bart looked me in the eye and told me, 'Maude, it's not about the bread. It's about Jesus. So get over it.' And I did. You will, too."

Heather wasn't sure if this made her feel any better. "It's not about the bread," she repeated, as if trying to convince herself that it really was true.

"Today, you get to watch," Maude said. "Why don't you pour yourself a cup of coffee and relax."

Heather did. She sat back and looked on as Maude poured just the right amount of flour into the center of the bowl and stirred in the other dry ingredients. Maude warmed the milk and melted the butter, then poured it in and began to stir. In almost no time, a large, doughy ball began to take shape in the big bowl. Maude floured her knobby hands, sprinkled a generous measure of flour onto the counter, and scooped the dough out of the bowl. Next, Maude began to knead—push, pull, turn; push, pull, turn. As Heather watched in wonder, a beautiful, soft, shiny mass took shape on the kitchen counter. The whole process hadn't taken more than 15 minutes.

"That's it?" Heather wanted to know.

Maude smiled and nodded.

"Now what?" the younger woman asked.

"Well, that dough is gonna rise, and I think we get to visit while your kids run Pastor Bob and José ragged." The two women laughed and talked. After a while, they checked the dough, and Heather gasped to see that the silken lump had grown into an immense, spongy mass, more than twice its original size. Maude punched it down, and then there was more kneading and waiting for it to rise. Finally, Maude brushed the loaf all over with a beaten egg and stepped back. "That's it, girl."

"Wow, Maude, you make it look easy," Heather admired as the bread disappeared into the oven.

As Maude and Heather had another cup of coffee, a wonderful aroma filled the kitchen. When the time was just right, Maude whisked the loaf out of the oven and gave it a smart rap on the bottom with an arthritic knuckle. "That hollow sound means it's ready," Maude explained.

Heather looked at the bread, so warm and golden on the counter, "Oh, Maude! It's beautiful!"

On the first Saturday of the next month, Heather and Maude worked together making the bread. They were a good team, and the younger woman learned quickly. In July, Heather tried it all by herself, with Maude looking on to give encouragement. It looked like the Presbyterian Church had, indeed, found a new baker.

As Heather got ready to drive home afterward, Maude stopped her. "Heather, you'll need these," Maude said, holding out the earthenware bowl and the wooden spoon. Heather looked into the bowl and saw that Maude had tucked an apron inside. Perched on top was the recipe. Maude said, "Now that you can do the baking, I'm taking a communion Sunday off for the first time in about sixty years. I'm gonna go visit my sister over in Cape Vincent. You'll do just fine. Here's my sister's phone number, just in case. But remember, it's not about the bread."

The first Saturday in August was the hottest day anyone could remember. The mercury topped eighty degrees, shot up to ninety, and didn't rest until it was over one hundred. There wasn't even the hint of a breeze to cool things down. Heather had a bad feeling as she stood at her kitchen counter with all the ingredients for the BREAD OF LIFE spread out before her. She started with the dry ingredients and then added the liquid. She stirred and stirred and stirred, but the more she stirred, the more things looked like a sticky mess. Heather began to improvise. She added a little more flour, and then she threw in a bunch of extra yeast and, for good measure, added a big handful of sugar. She pried the dough out of the bowl and began to knead, but the dough seemed more interested in sticking to her hands than sticking to itself. Sweat rolled down her back. Heather looked at the clock and was alarmed to see that an hour had passed and the dough wasn't looking any better.

When José came in with the kids and proposed a dip in Hoel Pond to cool off, Heather finally gave up, patting the dough into a huge, sticky, gluey ball and leaving it to rise on the counter. "It's not about the bread," Heather said to herself.

Heather didn't fully appreciate how bad it was until she got home. They opened the front door and were greeted by a strangely pungent, sour smell. When Heather shrieked and ran into the kitchen, she saw that the dough had risen to enormous proportions. Like the Blob, it had overflowed the countertop and swallowed up all items in its path. Heather punched it back and wrestled a saltshaker, a pacifier, and a bottle of Flintstones Chewables from its gooey grasp.

"It's not about the bread," Heather told herself, over and over again, as she battled the dough into something resembling a loaf and swabbed it down with egg. It was a relief when Heather slid the bread into the oven and closed the door. She fished some ice pops out of the freezer and took the kids into the yard to play in the shade while she tried to forget about what was lurking in the oven.

It was José who next raised the alarm, calling from the back door, "Honey, I think you better check this bread."

Heather rushed into the kitchen and threw open the oven door. The bread looked oddly lumpy and swollen. Parts were overflowing the baking sheet, as if trying to make an escape. "Oh, no!" Heather wailed as she pulled the baking sheet from the oven. Instead of the beautiful golden color of Maude's loaves, Heather's bread was mud colored and the bottom looked scorched. It was curiously shiny and profoundly ugly. José and the kids stood looking on in fear, as if expecting the bread to attack at any moment.

"I'll call Maude," Heather reasoned, "She'll come home and bake a new loaf." Before José could argue, Heather picked up the phone and dialed Maude's sister in Cape Vincent. She kept the quaver out of her voice until Maude got on the line, but as soon as she heard Maude's familiar hello, Heather began to cry, huge sobs shaking her shoulders.

"Heather, what's wrong?" Maude wanted to know.

"Oh, Maude!" Heather wailed, "I've killed the BREAD OF LIFE!"

Maude let Heather cry it out. "Honey," she said when Heather had grown quiet, "it's not about the bread." Heather sniffed. "Honey, the first time I made the BREAD OF LIFE, it looked like a big cow pie. It was dirt brown and dry as dust. Bart Rockwell told me that his dog got a hold of his first loaf, grabbed it right off the kitchen table; it was covered all over with slobber and teeth marks before he could retrieve it."

"Really?"

"Really. Heather, it's not about the bread."

Heather sighed, "I know that's what you've been saying, but Maude, if you could see this thing!"

"Don't 'But Maude' me, Heather. People come to church hungry on communion Sunday. It's not for the kind of bread that I bake, or Bart Rockwell baked, or even Elvie Smith baked. Folks are hungry for Jesus. They want meaning and purpose and love and truth. Heather, we can eat bread all day long, and no matter how beautiful or tasty or well-made it is, we'll still be hungry for all those things that truly make life worth living. There's only one real BREAD OF LIFE, Heather, and that's the Lord. That's the bread that people want on communion Sunday, and—in some way that I've never been able to figure out—that's exactly what they get. I think we could serve just about anything for the Lord's Supper—pita bread, matzo, rice cakes, even freezer-burned hotdog rolls—and folks would still come away satisfied."

Heather looked again at the huge, strangely shiny, misshapen loaf that had emerged from her oven. At least it wasn't a freezer-burned hotdog roll. She felt a little better. "Okay, Maude, thanks for the moral support. I know it's not about the bread, though if you saw how ugly this thing is, you might change your mind."

"You take care, Heather. Goodbye."

The next morning, Heather wrapped up her bread and took it to church. On the Lord's Table, shrouded in linen and nestled on the silver paten, it almost looked normal. But when it came time for the Lord's Supper and Pastor Bob uncovered the loaf, Heather thought everyone sat up a bit straighter, trying to discern exactly what was on the plate. Even Pastor Bob looked momentarily stunned. He quickly recovered, scooping the bread up and lifting it high in a sign of blessing and thanksgiving. There, as the bread was held aloft, floating in the golden light streaming through the rose window, Heather realized that her loaf looked exactly like a snapping turtle, swimming up from the depths of Hoel Pond in its dark, leathery shell. Unfortunately for Pastor Bob, the well-baked crust proved to be about as difficult to break as a turtle shell. While the congregation watched with mixed concern and amusement, Bob twisted and pulled and tugged until he finally had the loaf broken into four pieces, bundled into linen napkins, and handed off to four servers.

The bread passed through the pews, and as José turned to serve her with the words, "The body of Christ for you, my love," Heather finally knew that Maude Beecher was right. It wasn't about the bread. It was about Jesus, and Heather felt she had probably never needed Jesus as much as she did in that moment. She broke off a piece of the ugly turtle bread and ate, and in the eating she found that she got Jesus. Heather simply knew that God loved her and would never let her go, no matter how big a mess she made of the communion bread.

"I am the bread of life." Pastor Bob was back at the Lord's Table, quoting Jesus now. "Whoever comes to me will never be hungry, whoever believes in me will never be thirsty."

The following week, Heather ran into Maude in Green's Grocery. Maude was sporting a fuchsia Friends of the Cape Vincent Lighthouse T-shirt. Heather, as usual, had the Snugli plastered across her chest. Its occupant had just discovered her fingers and was trying to cram them all into her mouth at once. Maude smiled, "Heather, I see you survived communion Sunday."

"Oh, Maude!" Heather sighed, giving the older woman a hug that threatened to mash her infant. "The BREAD OF LIFE wasn't quite a cow pie, and it didn't have slobber and bite marks on it, but it looked an awful lot like a snapping turtle."

Maude paused a moment and tilted her head, trying to imagine it. "Now, Heather," Maude began, and the two women finished together, "it's not about the bread."

"You were right Maude. I didn't see it before, but it really is about Jesus. He can even bless us in something as ugly as a snapping turtle."

Maude smiled and nodded, "Amen."

Heather said, "Next month, I'll see if I can whip up something that looks like a northern pike, maybe serve it up on a lily pad."

"Sounds good, Heather. I'd like to see Pastor Bob's face when he gets a look at that," Maude added. The two women laughed and headed toward the checkout counter.

10

With One Voice

"May the God of steadfastness and encouragement grant you to live in harmony with one another, in accordance with Christ Jesus, so that together you may with one voice glorify the God and Father of our Lord Jesus Christ."

—ROMANS 15:5-6

B ob sat at his desk. He looked at the list of names and got that feeling that he often got when facing the perplexities of parish ministry. It was a sort of sinking, falling feeling in his gut, as if he were in a roller coaster car that had just come up over a high crest, only to plunge back down into the depths. "Am I crazy?" Bob said to no one in particular. He read through the names again: Eugenia, Chris, Heather, Betty Lou, Ernie, and Scratch. All had volunteered to be on the worship task force that would be reworking the Christmas Eve service.

Bob doubted that there could be six more different people. Eugenia Bergstrom was the perpetual chairperson of the worship committee. She had grown up in the church and never let anyone forget it. Chris Nelson, the youngest elder on the session, was best known for his shaved head, Hawaiian shirts, and pierced ears. Heather Rodriguez, despite having five children under the age of ten, baked the communion bread each month. Betty Lou Campbell was a fixture down at the Bluebird Diner and a master quilter. Ernie Leduc did double duty as both church member and sexton, ready to collect the offering or shovel snow at a moment's notice. Scratch Johnson had come to the church a few years ago after completing rehab at the local addiction treatment center. Scratch swore that Jesus kept him sober, and he never missed a Sunday. Eugenia, Chris, Heather, Betty Lou, Ernie, and Scratch? Forget finding a way to have them put together a service in harmony, with one voice to the glory of God, Bob thought glumly. He would be lucky if he survived the planning process. "Lord, have mercy!" Bob prayed.

For the first meeting of the worship task force, Bob thought he would gather folks for a potluck dinner. There was nothing like table fellowship to bring a group together; Jesus had been an expert at that. After dinner, they would simply read through the traditional service of lessons and carols that had been used to celebrate Christmas Eve for as long as anyone, including Eugenia Bergstrom, could remember.

That evening, as the task force arrived and Bob prepared to say grace, he looked over the dishes gathered on the buffet table and wondered if he had made a terrible mistake. There was a bag of beef jerky that he surmised came from Scratch. A colorful plate of sushi matched Chris's Hawaiian shirt. Ernie had brought his personal favorite—hot dog casserole. Sadly, Betty Lou had come directly from the Bluebird, armed with only half a coconut cream pie that looked like it had seen better days. Bob thought all was lost until Heather arrived at the last minute with an infant strapped to her chest and a big pot of her husband José's black bean soup. Everyone found something edible and they settled into the reading.

It went about as well as could be expected until the questions started. In her most reverent tones, Eugenia read the words of the angel Gabriel and young Mary from Luke's Gospel: "And the angel came in unto her, and said, Hail, thou art highly favored, the Lord is with thee: blessed art thou among women. And when Mary saw him, she was troubled at his saying, and cast in her mind what manner of salutation this should be."

"Whoa," Chris interrupted, "Came in unto her? Cast in her mind? What does that even mean?" Eugenia's mouth dropped open.

Scratch shook his head. "Beats me. They sure did speak funny back then."

Eugenia now looked apoplectic, so Bob quickly spoke up, saying the first words that came into his head. "Well, the angel Gabriel and Mary would have most likely spoken Aramaic or Greek."

Ernie Leduc, who wasn't happy that the meeting was cutting into Monday Night Football, said glumly, "It's all Greek to me, Bob."

"Can't we do something about this?" It was Heather now. Every head snapped around to where she was seated at the end of the table, but the men quickly looked away when they realized that, beneath a neatly arranged scarf, Heather was nursing her baby. "Why not find a way to tell the story in language that makes sense without an interpreter?" Heather insisted.

"Why not, indeed?" Bob wondered out loud. Now Eugenia was not only red-faced but speechless. "Betty Lou," Bob asked, "Would you pick up the reading from here?"

Later, Bob closed their meeting in prayer and sent them all home with an assignment—to continue to pray and consider how they could use their particular gifts to bring new life to their old Christmas Eve service.

Perhaps the best thing about the second meeting of the worship task force was that everyone came. Bob had to give Eugenia a lot of credit. When he asked if anyone would like to share their insights, Eugenia's hand shot into the air like a straight-A student. "I've been thinking, Bob. I'd like to take the lead on finding a new translation, something that is clear and easy to understand for young and old alike."

"Excellent!" Bob replied. "Who else has something to share?"

Ernie Leduc cleared his throat, "You know, folks, I've been thinking about the candles. Do you have any idea how much time I spend cleaning wax off the pew cushions and carpeting after Christmas Eve?"

"Ooh!" Heather weighed in, "I'm always afraid that my kids are going to set something on fire."

"Hey!" It was Chris now. "What if instead of candles, we got everyone to hold up their cell phones? There's this really cool flashlight app that you can download to make your phone shine." The thought of hundreds of cell phones in church, turned on, and glowing, made Bob nervous.

Betty Lou was the voice of reason. "People, what is wrong with you? You can't ask folks to give up their candles on Christmas Eve, but maybe you could look into another option for folks who worry about their kids or fire or the mess." It was agreed that Ernie would investigate the possibilities.

The sharing continued around the table. Betty Lou wanted to use her sewing skills to change up sanctuary decor. Scratch shared that Jesus had been so good to him that he wanted to make a special effort to promote the service in the community. Heather thought it would be nice to have communion—and why not have the children as servers?

Everyone but Ernie liked this. "Candle wax, bread crumbs, and grape juice," he lamented. "I guess I know what I'll be doing on Christmas Day."

No one was surprised that Chris Nelson's idea was the most unorthodox. "How about it, Chris?" Bob asked, "What has the Spirit been saying to you?"

Chris smiled broadly and his eyes lit up. Everyone leaned in to listen, but no one expected what came out of his mouth. With the same sort of reverence that Eugenia used to read the King James Bible, Chris intoned the word, "Didgeridoo."

"What?!" everyone said at once.

"Didgeridoo!" Chris answered, even more emphatic.

Eugenia, looking puzzled, said, "Dippity-do? We used to use that to style our hair. What does dippity-do have to do with Christmas Eve?"

Now it was Bob's turn to clear his throat, "I think Chris is talking about a musical instrument, the didgeridoo. It's a wind instrument from the aboriginal people of Australia. It sounds kind of, um, well, spooky and otherworldly."

"Yeah, buddy," Chris chimed in, "I just have this soundscape vision of the service beginning with a dark sanctuary, and then comes the sound of the didgeridoo, like the Holy Spirit blowing into our lives and bringing light."

Chris found an unlikely ally in Betty Lou. "Maybe I could help you with that light. I'm thinking about a star, like the Bethlehem star, all silvery and golden and shiny. Maybe the star can be lit as the didgeridoo finishes its song."

As the meeting broke up, Chris pantomimed puffing into his didgeridoo while Betty Lou talked about her star, and a shell-shocked Eugenia kept repeating, "Would somebody please explain what dippity-do has to do with the service!"

In the coming weeks, Pastor Bob and the members of the worship task force were busy, finalizing plans for Christmas Eve. True to her word, Eugenia Bergstrom made an exhaustive study of contemporary Bibles and settled on the Common English Version for its lively language and authoritative translation. In anticipation of Christmas Eve communion, Heather worked with the Sunday school class, teaching them about the Lord's Supper and giving them a lesson in bread baking. Scratch collaborated with Linda, the church secretary, to make fliers for the Christmas Eve service. He was seen handing them out everywhere, from Green's Grocery to AA meetings to the bowling alley. Betty Lou marched into Bob's office one day, after her morning shift at the Bluebird, armed with sketches and yard upon yard of fabric—silvery tulle, purple velvet so deep it was almost black, and gold netting that sparkled with sequins. Ernie placed an order for those glow-in-the-dark sticks, the chemical kind that kids like to loop around their wrists or link together to make necklaces. Chris and organist Frank Duncan were spotted most coffee hours with their heads together, undoubtedly cooking up musical mayhem.

Bob did his best to weave all those differing ideas into a cohesive service, but as Christmas Eve approached, he worried. Didgeridoos, gold netting, glow sticks? What had he been thinking? He began to fear a Christmas Eve catastrophe of epic proportions. With any luck, Scratch would have the pews packed with everyone in town to witness the insanity.

Bob wasn't alone in his anxiety. As word got out about the changes to the traditional service, Eugenia came to see him in his study. "Bob, I don't mean to rain on your parade, but I think you've got trouble on your hands."

Bob, who never liked to hear the word trouble, sat up straighter and pushed his glasses up on the bridge of his nose. "What do you mean, Eugenia?"

"Bob, folks won't have it. They don't want all these changes. You're making Christmas Eve into something strange and uncomfortable, and no one will like it. They'll leave the church—or they'll make you leave."

Bob looked at Eugenia, trying to figure out if he was being threatened. He probably was, but Eugenia looked so genuinely worried that he decided not to take it that way. He took a moment to gather his thoughts. "It isn't easy, is it?" he finally asked Eugenia. "To be in this church all your life and to love things just as they are—it doesn't feel very good to have that change. I know how hard this is for you, Eugenia. I'm grateful that you are willing to give people like Betty Lou and Heather, Chris and Ernie and Scratch a chance to share their gifts and creativity."

Eugenia looked away. Bob handed her a tissue. She blew her nose, dried her eyes, and said, "No, Bob, it's not easy. And I still don't understand what dippity-do has to do with Christmas Eve."

Bob smiled at Eugenia, "I'm not sure either, my friend, but I have a feeling that we are going to find out."

When Bob peeked out of the sacristy into the sanctuary on Christmas Eve, he didn't know whether to cheer or vomit. With his fliers and personal invitations, Scratch had drummed up a record crowd. Bob had never seen so many people in the church. They were packed into the pews like campers at Fish Creek on the Fourth of July. Bob pasted a smile on his face and hurried to the back of the church, where Chris Nelson was waiting with his didgeridoo. Bob noticed that Chris had dressed for the occasion. Instead of earrings, Chris had two Christmas ornaments hanging from his earlobes. A red and green Hawaiian shirt practically shouted "Happy holidays!" from beneath Chris's black leather jacket.

If Bob was nervous, Chris was not. "Pastor Bob!" the younger man greeted him, "Get ready for the Holy Spirit! This night is gonna rock!" Bob nodded, hoping that his panic wasn't showing, and hurried off to take his place on the chancel.

When the lights dimmed, the sanctuary fell silent, and worshippers sat up straight in expectation. Chris took a deep breath and began to puff and blow into his didgeridoo. When its strange, primordial, droning call leapt forth, all the hair stood up on the back of Bob's neck, as if an electric current had rocketed through his body. As the sound of the didgeridoo fell away, Betty Lou's star, all silvery and golden and magical, shone down from the top of the nave. For a moment Bob felt like he really was in Bethlehem, like a poor shepherd, joyous and dumbstruck by the heavenly host.

Years later, folks were still talking about that Christmas Eve service. Some said it was the year that the Holy Spirit finally showed up. Others claimed that, when the children served them communion, it was as if they were served by the Christ child himself. Ernie's glow sticks proved so popular with the young and the young at heart that he had very little wax to clean up the next day or in the Christmas Eves to come. Scratch insisted that so many people found Jesus and their sobriety that night that it almost put the Dew Drop Inn out of business. But Bob knew that the real miracle of that Christmas season was that those six very different people had found a way to glorify God with one voice.

11

Many Are Called

"For many are called, but few are chosen."

—MATTHEW 22:14

"Shall we pray our way out?" Pastor Bob asked. The nominating committee had pored over the membership rolls and pondered whom God might be calling to serve as an officer of the church. A slate of nominees had been chosen. Now, all that was left was the praying. Everyone obediently bowed their heads, and Pastor Bob closed the meeting: "Lord, we know that you have called men and women to serve you through this church. Send us forth to share your gracious invitation and open their hearts to the 'Yes' that you would have them speak; through Christ we pray. Amen."

At the far end of the table, Bob's youngest elder Chris Nelson jumped to his feet, his purple Hawaiian shirt practically glowing in the fluorescent light of the church hall. "Alright, alright, alright! I feel some yeses coming on! Let's do this thing!" Chris cheered, clearly trying to rally his less-than-enthusiastic troops. Over the years, the more seasoned members of the committee had heard more "Nos" to their invitations to serve than they cared to remember. All the same, as Chris headed out, they had to admire how much he loved being an elder and wanted others to join him in God's service.

As Bob walked with Chris to the parking lot, he asked, "What's your strategy, Chris?"

Chris paused in the cold, early autumn dark. He leaned against the side of his truck and pulled at his goatee, as he liked to do when puzzling over a question or pondering one of Bob's more obtuse sermons. He took out his list and read three names: Eugenia Bergstrom, Tubby Mitchell, and

Lenore Claiborne. "Hmm. Phone is too easy for people to say, 'No.' So, I'll do it in person, try to keep it personal, share from my experience. I'll start with Eugenia. I think she's most likely to say yes."

Bob grinned at Chris. "Sounds like a plan. Go get 'em, Chris," Bob encouraged before driving away, sounding more like a football coach than a pastor.

Chris extended his first invitation after church during coffee hour. Eugenia Bergstrom had served a number of terms on session and was a standing member of the worship committee, where she did her best to squelch Pastor Bob's kookier ideas. From across the church hall, Bob watched as Chris approached Eugenia. Today, Chris was in orange, his shirt a riot of bold tones that looked like the sun had exploded in his closet.

It didn't take a genius to figure out that things didn't go so well. Later, as Chris helped himself to a second cup of coffee, Bob sidled up to him, asking, "What did Eugenia have to say?"

Chris ran a hand over his shaved head and gave his goatee a tug, explaining, "Eugenia says she's been there and done that, I need to find new blood, and my shirt makes me look like a human pumpkin."

Bob commiserated, "Sounds like you got your first 'No,' buddy."

"Yeah," Chris agreed, "I just didn't think it would be so mean." This got the two men laughing and prompted a dirty look from Eugenia, who was surveying the mini quiches at the snack table. Strike one.

Chris used his lunch break to make his next invitation. On Monday, he went to the Good News Café, the local free lunch program where Tubby Mitchell often volunteered. Chris grabbed a tray and walked through the cafeteria line. Tubby piled his plate with string beans, mashed potatoes, brown gravy, and a grayish lump that Chris guessed was either Salisbury steak or meatloaf. Tubby promised to join Chris as soon as the rush was over and, sure enough, as Chris was mopping up the last of his gravy with a roll, Tubby took a seat across the table. "Good grub," Chris said by way of greeting.

Tubby shrugged off the compliment and tucked into his lunch. When Chris got around to the invitation to serve as an elder, Tubby listened thoughtfully before responding. "Son, that's awful nice of you to think of me, but I've got my hands full between work and the café."

Not ready to give up, Chris kept at it. "But Tubby, don't you think that your experience is needed at the session table? You could really help us think about better ways of reaching out to neighbors in need?"

Tubby chewed on this with a bite of meatloaf. "I suspect you're right," Tubby finally answered, "but it might cut into my fishing time." For the rest of lunch, Tubby regaled Chris with descriptions of his new ice auger and pop-up shanty for the coming ice-fishing season. Strike two.

Chris's final nominee, Lenore Claiborne, owned a kitchen store on Main Street. She was one of the best cooks in the village, and her ample figure suggested that she enjoyed tasting as much as she did cooking. A cheerful bell sounded when Chris entered the store, which smelled like apple pie and pumpkin spice. The shelves were chock-full with shiny kitchen gadgets of undetermined purpose. Near the cash register, a plate of fresh-baked goods looked tempting.

With his best smile, Chris approached the counter and helped himself to a cookie, which practically melted in his mouth. Lenore, whose nose had been buried in a cookbook, looked up with alarm. "Wow! This has got to be the best cookie ever," Chris began.

But before he got any further, Lenore said, "No!"

Chris knew Lenore wasn't talking about the cookie. This was beginning to feel personal. "Lenore, you don't even know what I have to say."

Lenore, closing her cookbook with a snap, declared, "I know why you're here, Chris Nelson. Eugenia Bergstrom warned me about you."

Feeling more like a criminal than the convener of the nominating committee, Chris persevered, "Lenore, we could really use your gifts for hospitality and business on the session. I'd be honored to work with you, and I can share that I've really grown as a person and a Christian in my time as an elder."

Lenore looked uncomfortable. Her round cheeks glowed pink and tiny beads of sweat dotted her upper lip. For a moment, Chris thought Lenore would relent, but in a blast of steely resolve, she shot him down. "Doesn't session meet on Tuesdays? That's the same night as my Weight Watchers meeting. I've made that commitment to myself, and I'm doing so well. Steve was just saying how proud he is of me. I owe it to myself to make that my priority. Sorry."

Lenore followed up with a bunch of stuff about points and personalized programs and weigh-ins that Chris didn't understand. Chris gave up and left, but not before Lenore talked him into buying a French press, a lemon zester, and a Ronco ROES Inside-The-Shell Electric Egg Scrambler. Strike three.

On Saturday morning, Chris drove to the church, feeling discouraged. He found Pastor Bob with Junior Miller, Charlie and Annette's boy. Born with Down syndrome, Junior was about twenty now and almost as round as he was tall. He had a shock of sandy, blond hair that was always falling in his eyes and a contagious joy for everything he did. Junior loved Chris and had taken to wearing Hawaiian shirts in an act of solidarity, even if it was, perhaps, a fashion choice ill-suited to his short, round frame. Bob and Junior were sorting through the dry and canned goods that folks had contributed to the food pantry. Junior checked expiration dates while Bob boxed things up.

Bob thought Chris looked a little careworn as Junior and Chris exchanged one of those funky handshakes that young people like these days. While Bob and Chris exchanged a more traditional grip, Bob asked, "Chris, what brings you here, looking like you lost your best friend?"

Chris shrugged out of his leather jacket and sighed, "Bob, I struck out. Three nominees, three big 'Nos'—I don't think anyone really even took my invitation seriously. I'm sorry, Bob. I feel bad for you and bad for the church."

Bob had served in parish ministry long enough to be well acquainted with the many ways that people say no. There was the outright no—some amused, some angry. There was the qualified no that usually begins with something like, "I would, but . . . " or "I might, if . . . " There was even the no that masqueraded as a yes—folks ordained as elders who never showed up to a meeting. Bob figured that all the times he had heard "No" brought him closest to knowing how Jesus truly felt—Jesus who had invited the world to come to his bountiful feast, only to be met with indifference, suspicion, and rejection from the very people whom God had sent him to minister to. Nothing that Chris told Bob surprised him, but he felt for the younger man and understood his disappointment.

When Chris finished, Bob asked, "Chris, why did you say yes to being an elder?"

Chris tugged at his goatee. "Well, I knew it wouldn't be easy. Between my job at the paper and a baby at home, my plate is full. But Nora and I talked about it, and she encouraged me to give session a try." Chris made a hands-up gesture, as if this said it all. "I guess I love the Lord, Bob, and I trust that God wouldn't call me to something that wasn't important for me and for the church. I know it was the right choice."

Bob rested a hand on Chris's shoulder. "I couldn't agree more, Chris. I think we just have to trust that you're not the only one who loves God and is willing to say 'yes' to the invitation."

Junior Miller had been listening closely. As Bob and Chris talked about next steps for the nominating committee, Junior spoke up, "I love the Lord."

It was true. Junior loved the Lord with a purity and intensity that took Bob's breath away. Whether Junior was raising money for shallow wells or helping out with Sunday school, he did so as if it were the most important thing in the world.

Bob looked at Junior's stubby form and decided that he couldn't think of anyone more deserving of a seat at the session table. "Well, well, well," Bob smiled, "many are called, but few are truly chosen. Chris, I think you have just successfully recruited your first elder. Congratulations to you both." Junior and Chris celebrated with another one of those fancy handshakes.

When Chris left, he looked lighter and more hopeful than when he had arrived. Bob and Junior returned to sorting food. They got a good laugh out of three cans of Del Monte fruit cocktail in heavy syrup—expired in 2002—that someone had decided to share with their neighbors in need. Bob suspected they had emerged from the dark recesses of Eugenia Bergstrom's pantry.

I hear that Chris is still out there looking for people who love the Lord. It's not too late to say "Yes."

12

Love One Another

"This is my commandment, that you love one another
as I have loved you."

—JOHN 15:12

By all accounts, Ulysses Lee McVicker was not an easy man to love. Most folks agreed that he was just plain mean, but they argued as to the cause of his disposition. Some said it was his name, Ulysses Lee, or Ulee for short. Who would name a baby boy after two army generals from opposing sides in the Civil War? It sounded like a recipe for inner conflict, not to mention plenty of schoolyard teasing. Some said Ulee was mean because of his war wound, shrapnel that lodged in his right buttock at the Battle of the Bulge. According to Ulee, his shrapnel wound—and just about everything else— was nothing but a pain in his ass. Others said that Ulee was mean because he had been unlucky in love, long ago jilted by a flighty gal who ran off with his younger brother. But most folks allowed that couldn't possibly be true because Ulee was just too unpleasant—too unlovable—to have ever entertained ideas about having a wife. He was such a hard man to love.

Ulee could be seen around town driving a beat-up truck that was a testament to a few too many mountain winters. The chassis was rusted through in places, and no one could remember if it had ever had a working muffler. No one parked near it because Ulee had a tendency to kick his truck door wide open, leaving a ding in the door of his neighbor. On the road, he was a speed demon, widely acknowledged as a menace to children and animals alike. Mothers shook their heads when they passed roadkill and said, "That Ulee McVicker has been at it again."

Ulee lived outside the village on his folks' farm. No one had worked it in years, and it was more than a little tumbledown, with peeling paint and a small armada of decaying farm equipment littering the yard. Over the years, a procession of mongrel dogs had populated the dog run, baring their teeth and warning off visitors. If you were brazen enough to walk right up to the front door and knock, you'd find yourself thinking that Ulee really needed to invest in a spittoon or stop chewing altogether.

Appearances can be deceptive. Despite his penchant for four-letter words and chew, Ulee was a church-going man. Every Sunday morning, he arrived at the Presbyterian Church five minutes before the service in a worn black suit and took his usual seat in the back row, a fresh coating of pomade holding his hair motionless. Woe to the visitor who accidentally sat in Ulee's pew—he was known to ask them to get up and move. When young Pastor Bob arrived, with changes to Sunday worship like sharing the peace of Christ, Ulee didn't like it. While others rose and turned to one another with smiles, Ulee simply stood, shooting black looks at anyone who might want to shake his hand or slap his back. Only Pastor Bob was brave enough to try that. Ulysses Lee McVicker definitely was not an easy man to love.

Ulee was a working man. For years, he worked the third shift, the overnight, at the mill. He always said he liked it because he didn't have to talk to anyone. Mornings, while the rest of town was rising and heading out to day jobs, Ulee would head home, stopping along the way at the Bluebird Diner for breakfast. That's where Betty Lou Campbell got to know him. Back then, she was a teenager, fresh out of high school, newly married, and waiting on tables. Every weekday, Ulee McVicker would sit at her table and order the same thing: two fried eggs, bacon burned, whole wheat toast with grape jelly, and black coffee, hot!

Now, Betty Lou prided herself on being a people person, able to draw out even the most reticent of patrons, but in Ulee she met her match. All her best pleasantries were met with an unvaried string of "Uh-huhs," with only a very occasional "You don't say." She'd sit up at night thinking of just the right thing to draw Ulee McVicker out of his shell and into the human race, but nothing worked. He'd eat his breakfast while ignoring her banter, and then he'd head home, leaving behind the same tip every time—five cents. That's right, a nickel. Now, this bothered Betty Lou, but no matter how hard she worked to improve her service—a bigger smile, a warmer greeting, hotter coffee, blacker bacon—the tip stayed the same.

Betty Lou was also Presbyterian. She knew that she should love her neighbor, but as time wore on, she found it harder and harder to love Ulee McVicker. She tried switching tables with other waitresses, to avoid Ulee, but the man had an uncanny ability to anticipate the switch and change his seat so that Betty Lou would have to be his server. The last straw came at the annual church mission sale, where Betty Lou sold beautiful hand-pieced quilts. How pleased she was when Ulee stood before her with a bright riot of colors cascading over his arms and pooling on the floor at his feet. Here at last was something to celebrate. "O, Ulee, what are you planning to do with my quilt?"

Looking from the quilt to Betty Lou and back, Ulee shrugged his shoulders and said, "Oh, it ought to make a nice blanket for my dog's bed, don't you think?"

Betty Lou imagined her lovely quilt covered with the hair and miasma of Ulee's latest mutt and her face flushed with anger. She took Ulee's money, carefully folded the quilt, and handed it to him with a sugary sweet "Aren't you thoughtful" that belied her inner rage. This whole loving-one-another thing was proving just a little more difficult than she had ever imagined.

When Betty Lou finally went to Pastor Bob for guidance, he listened carefully to all she had to say. Pastor Bob allowed that Ulee was a difficult case to love, most vexing indeed. "Tell me, Betty Lou," he asked, "have you thought about praying for Ulee?"

Betty Lou swallowed and blinked back at Pastor Bob. Praying for Ulee McVicker? This was truly not what she was hoping to learn from Pastor Bob. But that night, as she tossed yet another of Ulee McVicker's nickels into an old coffee can in her pantry, she said a little prayer. "Dear Lord, forgive me for my hard heart. Please bless Ulee McVicker and keep him in your tender care. Amen."

It wasn't the prettiest prayer in the world, but it was the best Betty Lou could do, and she found that she really meant it. Every night, as she squirreled away Ulee's nickels, she prayed, and with time Betty Lou found that she felt a little better about Ulee. That Pastor Bob was a smart one.

Things went on like that for a long, long time. Betty Lou continued to wait tables. When Ulee finally retired from the mill after more than forty years of service, they gave him a shiny, gold, old-fashioned pocket watch, and he wore it like a badge of honor, bulging in the breast pocket of his Dickies work shirt. When he retired, Betty Lou thought she'd finally get a break from Ulee McVicker, but it didn't work out that way. The day after he finished up working, Ulee showed up at the Bluebird at the same time, in the same work clothes, and ordered the same breakfast. And after breakfast? He left Betty Lou the same nickel tip. She continued to take the nickels home and put them in the coffee can with the same little prayer. Eventually, there were many nickel-filled coffee cans in the back of that pantry. Time passed and, apart from family and church, the one constant in Betty Lou's life remained Ulee McVicker with his burned bacon and nickel tip. He did not improve with age.

One Sunday in church, Betty Lou perked up as Pastor Bob taught about the Christian calling to "love one another." Pastor Bob preached about that great Reformer, John Calvin. Calvin himself had taught that our neighbors deserve our love and honor, even when they are worthless and contemptible, because they bear the image of God. This intrigued Betty Lou. Could even Ulee McVicker bear the image of God? Most folks agreed that he bore the opposite image.

After the service, as Betty Lou and her husband Dermott visited with Pastor Bob in the church hall, they looked over to see Ulee McVicker, swigging black coffee, eating all the donuts, and swatting at the children. Betty Lou sighed, "Pastor Bob, I guess John Calvin didn't know Ulee McVicker, did he?"

Pastor Bob began to nod in agreement but caught himself and asked, "How's that praying coming along, Betty Lou?"

"Oh, I'm wearing the Lord out, Pastor Bob," Betty Lou shared, "but I have yet to see any improvement."

Pastor Bob took a long look at Ulee and replied, "Sometimes the Lord works in subtle ways, Betty Lou. Keep up the good work."

One day, an early snowstorm blew through the county, dumping three feet of heavy, wet snow that pulled down power lines, snapped trees, and left roads slick with slush and ice. The Bluebird opened for business as usual, but for the first time in more than fifty years, there wasn't any Ulee McVicker at the table for breakfast. "That's odd," Betty Lou thought, but she chalked it up to the snow and the decrepit state of Ulee's truck. The old coot must have decided to sleep in rather than risk the roads with his bald tires.

That evening, Betty Lou paused in the pantry doorway; there wasn't any nickel from Ulee McVicker to toss into an old coffee can, but out of habit Betty Lou prayed just the same. "Dear Lord, forgive me for my hard heart. Please bless Ulee McVicker and keep him in your tender care. Amen."

The next morning, the sun was out and the roads had been cleared, but Ulee McVicker again failed to show up for breakfast at the Bluebird. Everyone joked that he must have decided to become a snowbird and fly off to Florida for the winter, but Betty Lou worried as she poured coffee and took orders. At break time, she asked Sal Cooper to cover for her, and she drove out to the McVicker homestead, her hand white-knuckled on the steering wheel. In the barnyard, the dog was missing from the run. Snow lay in a perfect blanket all around. Even Ulee's truck was wrapped in white. Betty Lou waded through the snow to the house and peered through the dirty windows—all quiet, too quiet.

"Ulee," she called out, raising a hand to knock. There wasn't any answer, except for the dog, which came hurtling out of a back room, looking anxious as he whined and pawed at the door. "Ulee!" Betty Lou opened the storm door and tried the doorknob. It turned easily in her hand and the door creaked open. "Ulee?" Betty Lou took a deep breath and went in.

She found Ulee in the living room. He was slumped over in his recliner. "Oh, Ulee!" Betty Lou cried, and his right eye flew open and looked right at her. His left side seemed kind of weak and droopy, and he couldn't speak. Betty Lou fished out her cell phone and dialed 911. Next, she called Pastor Bob. Then, she sat down next to Ulee McVicker. She held his hand, made small talk, and listened as the distant sound of sirens drew near. Betty Lou noticed that her hand-pieced quilt, bought long ago at the church sale, was draped across Ulee's lap, like a constant companion. The ambulance came and whisked Ulee away, and Betty Lou went back to work.

When her shift was over, Betty Lou checked in at home and then went down to the hospital. She found Ulee McVicker in a room, unconscious. He looked small and powerless, his body barely making a rise in the covers. Pastor Bob was there, seated next to the bed, reading scripture. Betty Lou noticed for the first time that Pastor Bob had gone gray and didn't look so young any more. He smiled as she pulled up a chair.

"Where are all the tubes and machines?" she whispered.

Pastor Bob answered softly, "Ulee has a health-care proxy on file, a written request not to use extraordinary means to prolong his life. It probably won't be long now."

"Oh!" Betty Lou responded, not really believing that Ulee McVicker would ever let go of his stubborn hold on life. "Well," she said, "I'll just wait here with him until his family and friends come to visit." Pastor Bob smiled.

They waited, but no one came. The hours stretched out and the shadows grew long and night fell, but no one came. They read scripture together, they prayed, and they visited, but no one came. Ulee McVicker's breathing grew labored, shallow, and infrequent, but no one came. Finally, Ulee stopped breathing altogether. They called in the nurse, who checked his pulse and shook her head, but still no one came. Pastor Bob took Betty Lou's hand, and he took Ulee McVicker's hand, and he prayed, asking God to take good care of their friend Ulee and welcome him home to his great reward.

Suddenly, Betty Lou found that her face was bathed in tears. First one, and then another great sob shook her body, and before she knew it, she was bawling, open-mouthed and snotty-nosed, right there in Ulee McVicker's hospital room. She stammered out an apology to Pastor Bob, "I am *so* sorry. I don't know what has come over me. I just can't believe that nobody came; I just can't believe that nobody loved him." With that, Betty Lou launched into a fresh series of sobs and wails, much to her personal alarm.

Pastor Bob closed his Bible. He took off his glasses and nodded his head. "There is nothing to be sorry about, Betty Lou," he said. "*You* came. *You* loved him."

Now, loving Ulee McVicker was a strange enough thought that it made Betty Lou pause in her sobbing. "I what?" she said.

Pastor Bob smiled. "You *loved* Ulee, Betty Lou. You served him, and you prayed for him for all these years. I call that love, and I think God would, too. Don't you?"

Betty Lou felt a little better. She looked at the mean old man there in the hospital bed, she squeezed his lifeless hand, and she thought about it. Finally, she shrugged her shoulders and said, "I guess I did love that old goat. I guess John Calvin was right after all, Pastor Bob. Even Ulee McVicker could bear the image of God. Even Ulee McVicker deserved some love and honor."

When Pastor Bob saw Betty Lou at church the next Sunday, he asked her how she was doing. "Well," she smiled, "breakfasts are kind of boring down at the Bluebird these days, but I think everything is going to be okay. You know all those nickel tips, Pastor Bob?"

He smiled.

"Well, I feel like I want to do something special with them," Betty Lou continued, "something Ulee would have liked."

"You do that, Betty Lou," he responded, wondering what in the world she could come up with that Ulee McVicker would have liked.

When spring finally came, they bulldozed the old McVicker place. Ulee's dog found a new home and was reported to be completely rehabilitated from any formerly vicious ways. Folks were a little less concerned about the safety of their children and pets because Ulee McVicker's rusty old truck no longer sped along village streets. There seemed to be a lot less roadkill out there.

One day, Pastor Bob stopped at the cemetery to pay his respects, and there he found Betty Lou, with her gardening gloves on and a trowel in hand, planting flowers at Ulee McVicker's grave. "Pastor Bob!" she beamed as he drew near. Betty Lou pointed to a modest, new, granite stone which marked Ulee McVicker's grave. "Look, Pastor Bob! What do you think about what I did with all those nickel tips?"

"A gravestone! Well, Betty Lou, aren't you full of surprises?" he said, smiling.

"Read it!" she encouraged.

Pastor Bob did just that. There, in simple block letters, the stone spelled out, "Ulysses Lee McVicker, 1923-2010," and below it in a graceful curling script was the simple inscription, "Love One Another."

"What do you think, Pastor Bob?" Betty Lou asked.

"'Love one another,'" he read, "That's what it's all about, isn't it? You've done well, Betty Lou. I think Ulee would have liked it just fine."

"I know it," Betty Lou said right back.

With that, Betty Lou returned to planting her flowers, and Pastor Bob wandered on to his next stop. Bob couldn't be certain, but he had a feeling that, right then and there, somewhere in heaven, Ulee McVicker just might have smiled.

"Love one another."

13

Everyday Worship

"Learn to do good; seek justice, rescue the oppressed,
defend the orphan, plead for the widow."

—Isaiah 1:17

Pastor Bob was so busy rubbernecking at events on the sidewalk that he nearly rear-ended the car in front of him. His aging Subaru groaned as he slammed on the brakes and made a sharp left into the village parking lot. He got out of the car and hurried up the block to where a small crowd was gathered in heated debate. At the center of the mob, two of his parishioners, Peter Bernard and Tubby Mitchell, were toe to toe, their faces flushed with anger. As Bob elbowed his way to the center of the scrum, he saw that Peter and Tubby weren't alone. Lined up with Peter were longtime church members Tommy and Kitten Stewart, as well as Lenore Claiborne. Standing firm with Tubby were his wife Irene and Scratch Johnson. They were outside the Good News Café, the local soup kitchen, which had been serving up free lunch for more than fifty years. Tubby's white apron, and the spoon that he brandished, proclaimed that lunch—and maybe more—was now being served.

Bob wedged himself between Peter and Tubby. "Friends, please! What's going on here?"

"This is what's going on here," Peter shouted, pointing to the front of his red T-shirt. It was emblazoned with the words, "The Good News Café Is Bad for Business." Bob noticed that everyone on his left, including Lenore, Tommy, and Kitten, wore the same shirt. They also carried signs. Some said, "Good News? No, Bad News!" and "There's No Such Thing as a Free Lunch!"

Lenore, who owned the kitchen shop across the street, spoke up. "Bob, I'm sick and tired of looking out of my store every day and seeing this," she said, gesturing to the cafe. "It's an eyesore, Bob. It's just plain bad for business. I've worked hard to make The Rustic Gourmet a success. Why should I have business driven away by something that looks like it belongs on The Bowery?"

Bob found himself wondering if Lenore had ever been to New York City, let alone The Bowery. Peter picked up the charge. "Bob, my store is just a few doors down. You know what I have to do, first thing every morning? Sweep up cigarette butts left behind by Tubby's patrons. I tell you, my customers spend big bucks in this village. They don't want to walk past the café and its collection of misfits."

Tubby must have taken that personally, because he growled, "Who are you calling a misfit?" He looked like he was about to give Peter a whack with his serving spoon, but, thinking better of it, he simply said, "C'mon, Bob. You know what Jesus taught about feeding hungry people. We're just being faithful servants here. Some people are just too self-interested and blind to see it."

Now it was Peter's turn to look offended; his jaw clenched and a vein pulsed alarmingly on his forehead.

Bob looked at the Good News Café. It probably hadn't been renovated since the 1970s. A dated wooden façade covered the original brickwork. The paint had peeled; the awning was threadbare and faded. The café's sign looked like it had been hand-painted by hippies—a smiling sun and rainbow arched over a big bowl of steaming soup. The cloudiness of the big front window suggested that the seal on the thermal glass had long ago been compromised. The sidewalk did, indeed, sport more than its fair share of cigarette butts. Bob was all about feeding hungry people, but the café looked seedy, nestled amid Main Street's tidy storefronts. Bob had to concede that, if he were a local entrepreneur like Lenore or Peter, he might feel that the café wasn't such a good neighbor.

Before Peter and Tubby could renew their hostilities, Bob asked, "Peter, have you ever eaten at the café?" Peter, who was by far the wealthiest merchant in town, looked at Bob as if he had two heads, so Bob pushed on. "I tell you what. I'm willing to mediate your dispute, but I want everyone with a red T-shirt on to have some lunches here this week. Get a feeling for what is going on. I'll join you. Then, on Sunday, we'll sit down after church and see if we can have a meeting of the minds. I'll provide lunch. What do you say?" The combatants reluctantly agreed to observe a truce until after Sunday's meeting.

True to their word, Tommy, Kitten, Lenore, and Peter showed up for lunch at the café the next day. Bob was relieved to see that they weren't wearing those red T-shirts, emblazoned with anti-café sentiment. As they passed through the cafeteria-style line, a tight-lipped Tubby served them—spaghetti topped with meatballs and marinara sauce; crusty, garlicky Italian bread; and a fresh green salad dotted with cherry tomato and cucumber. Then, they split up to take seats with other diners. Bob joined Lenore at a table of older women, including Maude Beecher from church.

Lenore took a seat, saying, "How nice to see you, Maude!" If Bob had worried that the conversation would be awkward, he was pleasantly disappointed. Maude made introductions and the ladies were soon chatting about how good the meatballs were and wondering what was for dessert. They shared family news and compared plots of favorite television shows. As they finished lunch, the older women all agreed to meet again next week—same time, same place. Bob walked Lenore across the street to The Rustic Gourmet. At the door, Lenore paused. "You know Bob, those women have been lunching together like that for more than a decade. Maude says that some of them still cook. Others get Meals on Wheels. But the café allows them to share a good meal together once a week."

"That's nice." Bob agreed.

The next day, Bob followed Tommy and Kitten through the cafeteria line. Tubby filled their plates with pot roast, mashed potatoes, and braised carrots. As they turned to find a seat in the dining room, Kitten looked confused. Several tables were occupied by children, mostly elementary-school age, tucking into their lunches with obvious appreciation. Tommy asked, "Bob, what's going on here?"

Before Bob could answer, Heather Rodriguez from church came to give them hugs, saying, "Come on over! I'm sure the kids would like to meet you." Bob spent lunch telling knock-knock jokes and guessing riddles, while Heather explained to the Stewarts that she sometimes brought neighborhood children for lunch in the summer months. "Half of our local kids qualify for free or reduced-price school lunches," she said. "In the summer, families may not have the resources to put lunch on the table. This is a way that I can help. Besides, Tubby keeps a stash of hot dogs in back for the picky eaters." Sure enough, several children were happily foregoing the pot roast to munch on hot dogs and potato chips.

If Lenore, Tommy, and Kitten had been moved by what they saw at the café, Peter Bernard remained resolute in his belief that the Good News Café was bad for business. Sure, Peter conceded, there were a few senior citizens and a smattering of children at the café. But in his view, most of the diners were what he called bums—men and women who looked like they had seen better days and were in need of a change of clothes, a trip to the barber, and a job.

But as fate would have it, on Friday, with his plate loaded with fish and chips and coleslaw, Peter sat down across from a familiar-looking, younger neighbor. About two bites into his haddock, Peter recognized him as Bruce the Juice MacLeod, once a talented speed skater and high-school friend of his son, Franco. The boys had signed up with the Marines and gone to Iraq right out of high school. Bruce had done four tours. When he finally came home, he was troubled, crippled by PTSD.

As Peter visited with Bruce, he thought about Franco, who didn't speak to him anymore. Peter looked across the dining room at Tubby and remembered that Tubby and Irene's boy, Todd, had come home from Iraq in a flag-draped coffin.

On Sunday, Pastor Bob was tempted to preach on the prophet Isaiah's bold indictment of the people of Judah, who worshipped God with elaborate ritual while neglecting their vulnerable neighbors—but Bob's wife Marge talked him out of it. Instead, he talked of Jesus's reminder that when we serve the "least of these," we are truly ministering to him. After church, the former combatants feasted on Bob's chili and cornbread. All words of anger were forgotten. Even Peter Bernard seemed to have lost his spark.

Bob shared a pan of Marge's apple crisp for dessert and broke the ice. "Well, folks, what do we think? Is the Good News Café bad for business? Tubby, surely even you can see that the café has seen better years. Maybe it's time to seek a less central location."

Kitten, who typically let Tommy do the talking, spoke up. "It seems that café is the heart of this village. What happens there at lunchtime is every bit as important as what we do here in church on Sunday mornings. I know it's an eyesore, but I'm willing to do some flower boxes out front—some pansies in spring, petunias for summer, evergreens in winter."

Tommy patted his wife's arm, suggesting, "Sweetheart, the café needs more than flowers."

Lenore spoke up in the awkward silence that followed. "The food sure is good. If you ever wanted to change your mission, Tubby, I think you could sell a lot of lunches to paying customers."

Tubby's brow furrowed, but before he could respond, Peter said, "Kitten's right. Maybe we should give the cafe a little of the vitality and prosperity that the rest of the downtown is experiencing. I can talk to other business owners. We could come up with a plan to give the café a facelift—and not just flower boxes. Get rid of the wooden façade, tuck-point the brick, paint, replace the windows and awning, make a garden out back for the smokers."

Lenore Claiborne was vigorously nodding. "Tommy," she said, "you're on the village board. Don't you think this is something they would be interested in sponsoring?"

Tommy agreed, "I think it's a possibility, especially if we partnered with local businesses and nonprofits. What do you say, Bob? Can the church kick in some resources?"

Bob thought about the church budget. The boiler should be replaced. The pipe organ needed repairs. The churchyard required grading and land-scaping. Money was tight. "Of course," he said, "I'm sure the church would love to help."

With that, everyone began talking at once. Voices were raised, not in anger, but in excitement as plans were hatched for the new and improved Good News Café.

Six months later, as the February snow was falling and a sub-zero wind blew up Main Street, Pastor Bob cut the ribbon for the dedication of the renovated café. They say it's still the best lunch in town.

14

Steadfast Love

"Happy are those whose transgression is forgiven."

—PSALM 32:1

"Can I come in?" The study door swung wide and there stood Joshua Howe, looking more like a linebacker than the convener of the church's AA group. The sleeves of his thermal shirt were pushed back, exposing an elaborate web of tattoos. The Van Dyck that perched between his chin and bottom lip was neatly trimmed. The angular slice of a scar bisected Joshua's left eyebrow, where he had once sported a ring.

"C'mon in," Pastor Bob called, waving Joshua toward the couch. The big man folded himself into a sit, his long, muscular legs stretched out across the carpet in a familiar sprawl. As Bob took a seat across from Joshua, he could feel himself entering an invisible cloud of Axe body spray, tobacco smoke, chewing gum, and worry. Bob took a closer look and noticed that his eyes were ringed with dark circles. Although Joshua wasn't a church member ("Not my thing, man"), Bob had found him to be deeply spiritual. In some odd and mysterious way over the past two years, Bob had become his pastor. Bob waited, expectant, wondering what had brought his young friend to his office early on a Tuesday morning.

Joshua, leaning in, proclaimed, "Bob, I'm going home this Easter." Now this was news. In two years, he had never once mentioned his family. Father, mother, grandparents, siblings—all were shadowy and amorphous figures, restless ghosts of his growing years down in Westchester County. Bob suspected that a decade of addiction had driven a wedge between Joshua and his kin. With two years of sobriety under his belt, maybe it was time to reconnect, but he looked more worried than happy about the prospect of a family reunion.

Bob nodded and tendered a neutral, "How do you feel about that?"

Joshua sat back and shrugged. "Man, where do I begin?" He tugged his shirt sleeves down to hide his tattoos and sighed, then out tumbled a long tale of broken trust and broken hearts. A family car wrecked in a drunk-driving accident at sixteen. Money stolen from his mother's purse to bankroll his addiction. Months spent using his grandparent's place as a crash pad after his father finally kicked him out. An overachieving sister, whom Joshua had spent years ignoring. A little brother, taken along and left behind at a keg party when he was just a twelve-year-old. Two failed attempts at rehab in an expensive, prestigious private facility. Lots of lies. Lots of broken promises. Lots of pain.

In working his Twelve Steps, Joshua had acknowledged his sins and made amends. His family had forgiven him, but Joshua still couldn't forgive himself. When he finally finished his long list of transgressions, he sat back, looking a little hollow and deeply grieved.

In the silence that followed, Bob could hear the tick of his desk clock and the roar of the boiler kicking on down in the church basement. Bob cleared his throat. "I hear you, Joshua. It sounds like you're carrying a heavy weight of guilt and shame."

Slowly nodding in agreement, Joshua responded, "Bob, you don't know the half of it. I don't sleep. I work out all the time to keep my mind off the past. I pray. I know it's time to move on, but man, some days, I can't face myself in the mirror. My past, Bob, it eats away at me. How do I sit down to Easter dinner like it's okay to start over?" Joshua's eyes took on a faraway look, like he was imagining that Easter dinner table—the spiral ham, the asparagus, the scalloped potatoes, the deviled eggs, the cut flowers, the family, and a tense silence, so thick that you couldn't cut it with a chainsaw.

Bob got an idea. He stood up and opened the study door. "Hold on a minute, Joshua. I'll be right back."

While Joshua sat brooding, Bob hurried to the other side of the church and began to root around in the sacristy cupboard. At the very back of the closet, Bob saw exactly what he was looking for. He reached in and brought forth the short, broad, shrouded form of the church's original baptismal bowl. It had rarely seen the light of day since the church had purchased an enormous, free-standing, wooden font back in the 1950s. As Bob pulled off its dark tarnish-resistant cover, the morning light bounced off the bowl's polished, silver surface. He took the bowl to the church kitchen, ran the tap until the water was just right, and filled it up. The bright water swirled to the top. A few bubbles glistened on its surface. As Bob balanced the bowl and walked back to the study, small waves lapped up and over the brim, leaving a damp trail on the carpet. Back in the study, Bob set the bowl on the coffee table, where it left a large, wet circle that he suspected would leave a white ring on the dark mahogany.

Now it was Joshua's turn to question, "What's up with that?"

Bob smiled. "That, my friend, is the church's baptismal bowl. It was given to the church in 1859. For more than a century, ministers used water from this bowl to baptize babies and new Christians." Bob reached forward and poked a finger in the water, causing ripples to bounce out to the rim and back. "Sometimes, I like to think about all the people who have been touched by these waters, who were claimed at this font as beloved children of God." Joshua and Bob both leaned forward and peered into the bowl, as if by doing so they could see into the past.

Bob reached a hand down into the water and it rose perilously close to the rim. "I imagine that those generations of people did all kinds of things. Some were farmers. Some were shop owners. I'm sure there were more than a few homemakers. Probably doctors, loggers, bookkeepers, teachers, nurses, boat builders, guides, lawyers." Bob scooped the water up and allowed it to slip between his fingers, back into the bowl. "Do you know what they all had in common, Joshua?"

Joshua's brow furrowed as if he were trying to make sense of something that was just beyond his grasp. He sat back and shrugged.

Bob smiled a little rueful smile, "Joshua Howe, like me, like you, they were all sinners. God's people make bad choices, go down wrong paths, turn away from God, do hurtful—sometimes horrible—things, even to the ones they love. That's the way things are."

Bob noticed that the younger man's breath had caught, waiting to hear what Bob would say next. Bob reached his hand back down into the bowl. This time the water did spill over, running out on the table and dripping over the edge to pool on the rug below. "Here's the thing," Bob continued. "These waters remind us that, despite our sinfulness, God has claimed us as God's children. God chooses to love us, even when we are hard to love, Joshua. God's steadfast love surrounds those who trust in him."

With that, Bob pulled his hand out of the water. He reached across the table and made the sign of the cross right on Joshua's forehead, just a little north and west of that scar from the eyebrow ring. "Joshua," Bob said, "it's time to begin again. Know that you are truly forgiven and be at peace." The big man's eyes filled with tears. Bob looked down and mopped up some of the mess he had made while Joshua caught his breath. When Bob looked back up, the tension had gone out of Joshua's body. He seemed more at ease than he had ever been in the two years that Bob had known him.

The two men sat in silence for a few moments. When Joshua spoke up, his voice sounded lighter. "You know, Bob, my mom sings in the choir of our church back home."

This really didn't surprise Bob at all, but he said, "You don't say."

Joshua stood up. "Yeah, well, maybe I'll even go to church this Easter, if you don't think the roof will fall in."

Bob stood and laughed, thinking how nice it would be to see Joshua in a church pew somewhere down in Westchester County. "I think the Lord would like that, Josh."

Joshua reached out to shake Bob's hand. "Thanks, Bob," he said, giving an extra squeeze that spoke of gratitude and possibility.

Bob gave a little squeeze back. "Safe travels, Josh. Go with God, my friend."

That was the last time that Pastor Bob saw Joshua, but every now and then, round about Easter, Bob gets a greeting card from down Westchester County way. Some years the card sports bunnies and chicks. Other years, Jesus makes an appearance, hovering outside the empty tomb. Once, Bob got one of those musical cards. When opened, it played Händel's "Hallelujah Chorus." Whatever the card may look like, the message inside is always the same, written in bold letters—"God's steadfast love surrounds those who trust in him."

15

Provoke and Encourage

"And let us consider how to provoke one another to love and
good deeds, not neglecting to meet together, as is the habit of
some, but encouraging one another, and all the more as you
see the Day approaching."

—HEBREWS 10:24-25

M alaise might have been the best word to describe it. Bob had been at
the Presbyterian Church long enough to preach through the three-
year lectionary cycle a few times when it came to his attention: a spirit of
discouragement. That's how it made him feel whenever he saw it in action,
as if the energy and good will had been sucked right out of him, leaving him
down and depleted, and even a little grumpy.

The spirit of discouragement first hit the sexton, Ernie Leduc. Ernie
was a hardworking, humble man who delighted in a job well done. Every
week, in anticipation of Sunday morning, Ernie was busy about the church
getting things ready. He vacuumed, polished pews, and filled the liquid
candles. He buffed up the big brass cross with an especially soft, deerskin
chamois until it gleamed in the soft light of the stained-glass windows.
Early each Sunday morning, Ernie would get out a small metal comb and
patiently straighten the fringe on all the paraments. Then, he would turn on
the sound system, adjust the overhead lighting, and take a moment to sit in
the still and empty sanctuary, knowing that all was ready and he had played
his part to the best of his ability.

Over the years, Ernie had learned that, no matter how attentive his
weekly efforts might be, there were always a few complaints to face each

Sunday. Comments were generally passed to Eugenia Bergstrom, the worship committee chairperson, who made a habit of compiling a list and presenting it to Ernie during coffee hour fellowship. The list would say things like: "cobweb spotted on organ pipe," "pews too lemony," "not enough t.p. in women's room," or "ribbons dangling from hymnal in third pew." Ernie would take his list with a smile and put it in his pocket, where it would stay until he accidentally ran it through the washer and drier later that week.

But one Sunday, as Eugenia handed over the list, Ernie's heart sank a bit, even though the list only had one item on it—"flame on one candle one-half inch shorter than other candles." Ernie looked at the list, and he then looked back at Eugenia. A sad look of defeat settled across his long face, and a frown tugged down the corners of his mouth and creased his leathery cheeks. He tucked the note into his pocket, put down his coffee cup, pulled on his parka, and went home.

Ernie was not the only one to feel the grip of that discouraging spirit. When it came time for the mission committee to hold their annual fundraising dinner, they discovered that, although the harvest was plentiful, the laborers were few. Just about everyone they asked to help was too busy—with work. parenting, civic commitments, or travel—to get involved. When the committee chairperson, Maybelle Howard, told Pastor Bob the bad news, Bob tried to put a positive spin on it. He talked about the virtues of sabbath and taking a year off to refresh the weary heart, but Maybelle felt discouraged all the same, as if she had personally let her pastor down.

It wasn't just mission volunteers that were hard to come by. No one wanted to teach Sunday school. When asked, folks argued that they had just taught the year before, or they were allergic to children, or they really didn't know their scripture. Folks on the Christian education committee felt disappointed and overwhelmed. It was rumored that the spirit of discouragement was even spreading to the Sunday school classes. The nine-year-olds, led by Jackie Carl, who had moved permanently to his grandmother's house, were plotting an agnostic coup and wanted to replace the annual Christmas pageant with "Waiting for Godot."

Even the typically intrepid choir felt the touch of that discouraging spirit. Frank Duncan, the organist, reported to Bob that the pipe organ had begun to make an odd, intermittent, rustling, wheezing, squeaking noise that could only mean one of two things—demon possession or expensive repairs ahead. Pastor Bob had a bad feeling that an exorcism was not going to remedy the situation. The choir, fearing that the organ could belch or die at any moment, came to midweek practices with a certain justifiable reluctance that did not make for inspired Sunday singing.

Pastor Bob, like many in his profession, had a few strategies for responding to church malaise. Chief among his arsenal of ministerial tools was "setting a good example." Bob reasoned that if you can just be the best shepherd that you can be, the sheep are sure to feel inspired to do the same. He liked to think of it as contagious leadership, but lately Bob wondered if folks had developed some strange immunity to his shepherding wiles. When he had tried to convince Maude Beecher to take a turn at Sunday school leadership, she had stopped him midway through his invitation, exclaiming, "Pastor Bob! What you're selling, I ain't buying. Uh-uh!"

Bob had to switch to Plan B: "stepping up." That meant temporarily taking on extra duties to help the congregation over the rough spot until others were motivated to do a little stepping up of their own. Boy, did he ever step up. Pastor Bob instituted a Monday morning staff meeting to build morale. But no matter how much Colombian coffee Bob brewed or how many apple fritters Bob supplied, Ernie Leduc didn't seem to feel any better about his job. Pastor Bob reorganized the church committee structure, scheduled potluck committee nights, and led special inspirational retreats, but no one new heard the call to service. Pastor Bob talked his wife, Marge, into teaching Sunday school. In a moment of real desperation, he even convinced his teenage son Paul to take a turn as the nursery attendant, but the Christian education committee still couldn't find enough teachers.

As Advent hurtled on toward Christmas, Bob wrote a new post-existentialist play for the Christmas pageant in which shepherds and angels who were waiting for Godot discover that he was already in their midst. But when the nine-year-olds read it, they didn't like it one bit and threatened to burn down the manger. Pastor Bob even launched a "Save the Organ" capital campaign and made a generous financial gift to inaugurate the fundraising effort. But a few misguided alarmists in the congregation, led by Tommy and Kitten Stewart, spread rumors that there was a secret plot afoot to do away with the organ and bring in a praise band, and all the traditionalists threatened to leave the church.

No matter how much Pastor Bob tried to set a good example, and no matter how much he stepped up to the plate, the spirit of discouragement would not let go of the church. In fact, the more he did and the less he seemed to achieve, the more Bob felt discouraged, depleted, and down in the dumps. He hit a low point one snowy evening near Christmas as he climbed into his car to head home. He slipped the key in the ignition and turned it over, only to discover that his battery was completely dead—wouldn't even hold a jumpstart. Even Bob's Subaru had had all the energy sucked out of it. "Lord," Pastor Bob prayed, his head bowed against the steering wheel as he waited for Tubby Mitchell to roll up in his tow truck, "I could use a little encouragement right about now."

Next morning, when Pastor Bob arrived at the automotive shop to pick up his car, Tubby Mitchell invited him to sit for a cup of coffee and a visit. They talked about the impending demise of the pipe organ, the challenges of rebellious nine-year-olds, when there might be enough ice to drag the shanty out for a little fishing, and what to get Irene for Christmas. When Bob stood up to leave and fished his wallet out of his coat, Tubby waved him off. "This one is on me, Pastor Bob. You keep up the good work."

Then, when Bob got into his car, he saw that Tubby had left one of Irene's excellent, homemade apple pies on the passenger seat. A little hand-written note had been left on top of the aluminum foil covering, a few lines of scripture copied out in a careful hand: "Do not fear, for I am with you; do not be afraid, for I am your God. I will strengthen you, I will help you, I will uphold you with my victorious right hand." Bob blinked and looked back into the automotive shop where Tubby stood smiling and waving goodbye. The spirit of discouragement that had weighed so heavily on Pastor Bob's heart lifted. He felt filled with energy, life, and an irresistible urge to sing a few verses of "How Great Thou Art."

All the way back to the church, Pastor Bob thought about what Tubby had done for him—a listening ear, a generous act, some home-baked goodness, and the promises of scripture. Maybe Bob didn't have it quite right. Maybe people weren't looking for a good example and an overworked pastor to get inspired. Maybe they needed a little provocation. It was worth a try.

Later that day, when Ernie Leduc dragged out his especially soft chamois to polish up the cross, he found his very favorite sweet treat waiting for him on the Lord's Table—a Terry's Dark Chocolate Orange, all shrouded in gold foil, ready to be whacked and cracked and nibbled. Tucked into the square box was a sticky note with words from the prophet Isaiah: "Those who wait for the Lord shall renew their strength, they shall mount up with wings like eagles; they shall run and not be weary; they shall walk and not faint." As Ernie snacked on the chocolate and buffed up the brass, he felt energized for the first time in months. He forgot all about Eugenia Bergstrom and her lists. He remembered instead the goodness of God, who is faithful, who renews the strength of those who wait.

On Saturday morning, when the children of the church gathered for the final dress rehearsal of the Christmas pageant, they learned that a few last-minute changes had been made to the play. Pastor Bob had written a new part for the nine-year-olds: black sheep. They got to wander around in a group looking lost and singing "O Come, O Come, Emmanuel." Best of all, they would wear black pajamas with hoods, which with only a little imagination made them look like ninja warriors. By the time rehearsal was over and the pizza had arrived for lunch, all the kids—even the nine-year-olds—were convinced that this was perhaps the best Christmas pageant ever. They couldn't wait to share it with the congregation.

On Sunday morning, Ernie Leduc arrived early, as usual. He combed the paraments, adjusted the lights, and turned on the sound system. He took a seat in the sanctuary and thanked God for renewing his strength.

All the nine-year-olds arrived extra early, swarming into the Sunday school room, donning their black-sheep costumes, and practicing their ninja moves. Karate chops and roundhouse kicks were syncopated with musical pleas to "ransom captive Israel."

As the choir rehearsed, the organ wheezed and gasped its way through the anthem—this one with a particularly enthusiastic bass line. When Frank Duncan got ready to make another go of it, Eugenia Bergstrom called for silence, "Hush up, there! What's that?"

Every ear strained to listen as a new sound emerged from the pipes. It started out faint, like the threat of a fingernail against a chalkboard. Then, when Frank gave a key a poke, it got real loud, real fast.

Eugenia was the first to move, hiking up her choir robe and yelling, "Run!"

A free-for-all ensued—sopranos, altos, tenors, and basses made a mad dash for the imagined safety of the nave. Only Frank Duncan stayed put, transfixed by the growing din. As the choristers scattered, he gave the keyboard another tentative poke. A terrible, rattling, scrabbling, shrieking noise was followed by a tense silence.

"Look-it!" one of the ninjas yelled, pointing to the mouth of the largest brass pipe. A small, triangular, black face with bright eyes appeared. It was soon followed by a furry body with leathery wings. Amid the shrieks of Eugenia Bergstrom and the laughter of the nine-year-olds, a bat launched itself into the sanctuary air. A bold Ernie Leduc dimmed the lights and took off in hot pursuit. He eventually swaddled the bat in his jacket and whisked it off to safety.

Freed of its unwelcome guest, the pipe organ was restored to full-throated glory, rattling the windows, shaking the floor joists, and prompting Maude Beecher to turn down her hearing aids. Later, the children did such a remarkable job with the Christmas pageant that every adult in worship that day felt inspired to help out in Sunday school, and they never had a teacher shortage at the Presbyterian Church ever again.

After church, as folks gathered in the great hall for coffee-hour fellowship, Pastor Bob noticed that the spirit of discouragement that had oppressed the church seemed to have lifted. For the first time ever, Eugenia Bergstrom didn't have a list for Ernie Leduc. Instead, she lavished him with praise for his previously undiscovered bat-catching gifts. The nine-year-olds had had so much fun playing black sheep that they refused to take off their costumes, and it's rumored that some even wore them to bed that night.

When Pastor Bob wandered back to his study to take off his robe, Tubby Mitchell caught up with him. Bob thanked Tubby again for the work on his car, the apple pie, and the encouragement. "Don't mention it, Pastor Bob," Tubby said. "It was our joy to get your batteries recharged. Doesn't scripture tell us to be encouragers, to provoke one another to love and good deeds?" The two men smiled at one another and nodded.

"Say, Tubby," Pastor Bob wanted to know, "what did you think of the Christmas pageant?"

"Good stuff. Those black sheep, lost and longing—very provocative." Tubby answered.

"I think Jackie Carl and the other nine-year-old rebels would agree," Bob laughed.

Tubby thought a moment. "I'm not sure why, Pastor Bob, but I found myself thinking that, since I'm almost retired, I could probably take a turn as an elder. What do you think?"

Pastor Bob's smile got even bigger. "Well, Tubby, I think that sounds downright encouraging. Let's talk about that some more."

While Ernie Leduc departed to seek a new home for the bat, and the Christian education committee went down to the Bluebird for a celebratory lunch, and the black sheep made a play date for later that afternoon, Tubby Mitchell and Pastor Bob had a second cup of coffee and began to talk church leadership.

16

Washed

"Then he poured water into a basin and began to wash the disciples' feet and to wipe them with the towel that was tied around him."

—John 13:5

P astor Bob should have known he was in trouble when he told his big idea to the worship committee. In the stunned silence that followed, he looked around the conference table. Eugenia Bergstrom's eyebrows had shot right up to her hairline in shock. Frank Duncan, the organist, snorted and feigned an intense interest in his notes. Heather Rodriguez's mouth hung open in disbelief. It wasn't exactly the enthusiastic response that Bob had anticipated.

Heather spoke up first. "You mean to tell me that Jesus actually washed peoples' feet?"

Bob smiled. "Yes, Heather, at the Last Supper, before he broke the bread and lifted the cup, Jesus washed his friends' feet. It was his way of telling the disciples that those who followed him must be servants."

Heather seemed to take this in with mixed awe and disgust. "Foot washing? Wow!"

Eugenia Bergstrom cleared her throat, inquiring, "Pastor Bob, isn't this foot washing something that the Baptists do?" The very slight hesitation that preceded "Baptists" told Bob that Eugenia didn't think much of Baptists, or foot washing. Bob was ready, though, as he opened his *Book of Common Worship* and slid it across the table, tapping the spot in the liturgy for Maundy Thursday that called for foot washing. Eugenia's face fell. She whipped out her reading glasses and scrutinized the page in disbelief.

Eugenia wasn't ready to give up. "We've never done this before. Why would we start now?"

Bob sighed, thinking of all the times that he had heard those words in his years of parish ministry. "Well, Eugenia, I hear your concern, but I think foot washing gives us a chance to be a little like Jesus amid the darkness of Holy Week. It puts us on our knees in self-giving love. I know it's new for us, but I think it could be a powerful lesson in following and serving the Lord." Bob hadn't changed Eugenia's mind, but he felt he had given her something to think about.

Organist Frank Duncan took advantage of Eugenia's silence. "Bob, I'm assuming this service will be in the church hall?" Bob nodded and began describing how he imagined setting the scene for worship—candlelight, basins, ewers, towels. When Bob paused, Frank spoke up, "Well, Bob, if the service is in the hall, you won't need me on organ." It might have been Bob's imagination, but Frank seemed to look relieved, as if he had narrowly escaped some terrible, deadly contagion. Bob made a note to ask his wife Marge if she would play piano on Maundy Thursday.

At dinner the next night, Bob told Marge and their son Paul all about his Maundy Thursday plans. When Bob got to the part about the foot washing, Paul, who was in the middle of taking a drink, began to laugh so hard that milk shot right out of his nose. When Paul had recovered enough to speak, he said, "Sorry, Dad, but, dude, you seriously cannot be thinking about having people wash other people's feet. That's, like, totally repulsive."

Bob had never thought about foot washing from Paul's perspective. "What do you mean, Paul? I think if Jesus did it, we can give it a try."

Paul was having none of it. "Whatever, Dad. You go for it, but I'm definitely not touching anyone's heinous feet. No way."

Later, as Marge and Bob cleaned up in the kitchen, Marge laid a hand on her husband's arm. "Honey, I'm in your corner. Sign me up for piano playing, but are you sure about this Maundy Thursday service?"

Bob sighed. He was beginning to get that sinking feeling that seemed to accompany much of his ministry. Why was it that so much of following Jesus felt like falling down, or swimming against the tide, or herding cats? For a moment, Bob's vision for a foot-washing service wavered. Bob patted Marge's hand, confessing, "I want to give it a go, even if we never do it again."

"Okay," Marge said, sounding skeptical. "I'd better give Donna a call." Donna was Marge's friend who worked as a beautician.

"Oh, are you thinking Donna might want to come to the service?"

"Not really, but if someone has to touch my feet, I'm investing in a good pedicure."

In the following weeks, Bob promoted the foot-washing service. He made some colorful flyers that showed Jesus washing his disciples' feet. He prepared a calendar notice for the newspaper and radio station. He put an enticing announcement in the bulletin and wrote an inviting article for the newsletter.

As Bob was finishing up his article, he heard a knock at the door to the pastor's study. "C'mon in!" he shouted.

The door cracked open and Eugenia Bergstrom's head poked around the corner, soon followed by her body and a big plate of cookies. "Why, Pastor Bob, I just thought I'd come by and share a little of my baking with you. You take these home to Marge and Paul. I know how much that boy loves my chocolate-chip cookies."

Bob knew a bribe when he saw one. He had had a feeling that it would take more than one discussion to win Eugenia over to the foot-washing cause, but he had never imagined that she would resort to cookies. Eugenia took a seat, placed the cookies on the desk, and peeled back the plastic wrap. "Eugenia," Bob sighed, "is this about the foot washing?"

Eugenia's cheeks flushed a guilty pink. "Bob, are you sure about this Maundy Thursday service? Why the foot washing? I've been thinking a lot about this, and I don't see why we can't do a hand washing. It seems much more hygienic and I—er, I mean we—wouldn't have to touch anyone's feet."

Pastor Bob nodded his head and reached out to take a cookie. He took a bite while he mulled over Eugenia's idea. "Hand washing instead of foot washing? Well, I can see where that might make some people a little more comfortable." Eugenia began to look hopeful. "But here's the thing, Eugenia, Jesus didn't wash hands at the Last Supper. He washed feet, grubby feet that wore sandals all day and walked dusty, unpaved roads. I think Jesus wanted his friends to do what he did, regardless of whether it made them feel comfortable or uncomfortable. In fact, he said, 'Whoever serves me must follow me, and where I am, there will my servant be also.'"

Eugenia looked defeated. She reached across the desk and grabbed a cookie. "Darn that Jesus," she said, and took a big bite.

On Maundy Thursday, Pastor Bob helped the sexton, Ernie Leduc, set up chairs in the church hall. Bob found a basin and ewer in the furthest recesses of the sacristy. He created a foot-washing station—two wooden chairs, a small table decked with an oil lamp, and a homespun linen cloth. On the floor between the chairs, he placed the basin and the ewer. Bob decided to wait until just before the service to fill the pitcher, so that the water would be warm and comforting. When everything was in place, Bob surveyed their work, hoping that the Lord would be pleased.

When Marge arrived before the service to warm up on the piano, she had a slightly pained expression. Bob assumed that the source of the pained look was Paul. Marge had somehow gotten their teenager to attend, but Paul didn't look excited about it. "Glad you could make it, son!" Bob said.

He tried to give the boy a hug, but Paul pulled him up short with his hand and the words, "Whatever, Dad." Paul slunk into the back row of chairs, pulled out his phone, popped in his earbuds, and pretended to be just about any place other than the church hall.

"Don't worry about him," Marge said. "On the way here, he actually asked me some questions about the service and seemed interested, even if it wasn't in a way that either of us would appreciate."

"Well, thanks for the support," Bob answered, giving Marge a quick hug. As she turned to head for the piano, Marge winced. "Are you alright, Marge?"

"Ugh! It's my feet. They look great, but Donna must have taken off three layers of skin. I feel flayed." As she sat down behind the piano, Bob guessed that Jesus had never had to comfort one of his disciples for an overly aggressive pedicure.

Next to arrive was Heather Rodriguez, enjoying a rare night out without the whole family. Heather told Pastor Bob that her husband José had actually offered to stay home and take care of all the kids when he heard that the service would involve foot washing. Wasn't that thoughtful of him? Not long afterward, Eugenia Bergstrom arrived. She didn't look happy, but Bob had to give her credit for being there. When he waved to her, she pretended that she didn't see him. She sat down in the back row, not too far from Paul, and immediately made him turn off his phone. If Eugenia was going to suffer through this, she wanted company.

Pastor Bob filled the ewer as the time for the service drew near, but the seats remained empty. Marge launched into the prelude. Only one more worshipper arrived, Ralph Beecher, Maude's brother, who was perhaps the most intensely private member of Bob's congregation. Ralph walked with a pronounced limp and leaned on a cane. Although Bob had never been able to get Ralph to talk about his disability, Bob suspected that it had something to do with his military service. Ralph had been part of the D-Day invasion. He was the last person whom Bob had imagined would come to the service. Bob shook Ralph's hand. "Ralph! Thanks for coming. I hadn't figured you for a foot-washing enthusiast."

Ralph smiled. "Pastor Bob, I'm not sure how I feel about foot washing, but I support you." Ralph took a seat as Bob headed up front to lead worship.

When the time came for foot washing, Bob invited folks to come forward in pairs and take turns washing one another's feet. Marge began playing all those beautiful Holy Week hymns, "Ah, Holy Jesus!" and "Were You There?" and "O Sacred Head, Now Wounded," but no one moved to the foot-washing station. Bob decided he had better go first. He walked over to Ralph Beecher and asked, "Brother Ralph, won't you join me?"

The men took seats in the wooden chairs. They rolled up their sleeves and rolled up their pants. They stripped off their shoes and socks. Bob knelt down in front of Ralph and lifted up the ewer of warm water, but he froze as he looked at Ralph's feet. Make that foot, because Ralph Beecher only had one foot. It was perfectly ordinary—with hairy toes, thick calluses, and well-trimmed nails—but the other foot and the lower leg, poking out of the bottom of Ralph's rolled up trousers, were definitely prosthetic. Bob stared at those mismatched feet and wondered how this private, quiet, guarded man had found the courage to come to a foot washing and take his place at the front of the hall for everyone to see.

Ralph spoke up, "You probably only need to wash the real one, Bob." Bob placed Ralph's foot in the basin, poured water over it, and gently toweled it dry. Next, Bob took Ralph's prosthetic foot, placed it in the basin, and washed and dried it with equal gentleness and love. When Bob was done, Ralph washed Bob's feet, and for just a minute, Bob could have sworn he saw Jesus there in the lamplight, on one knee and pouring out the water.

When Bob had helped Ralph back to his feet, Heather brought Eugenia to the front of the hall. The women washed one another's feet. They wept and embraced. Next, Paul slouched forward and stood by his mother's side as she finished "Go to Dark Gethsemane." Then, mother and son moved to the foot-washing station and washed one another's feet in silence. Paul thought about his mother washing his feet as a baby and how nice it was to be able to do this for her. Marge later claimed that she had a healing that night. As Paul washed her flayed feet, they miraculously grew three new layers of skin, and she left the church ready to dance. Instead, they stopped and had pizza.

When Bob got home later, the message light was blinking on the answering machine. He pushed the playback button and listened to Eugenia Bergstrom's voice. "Bob? It's Eugenia. I was just thinking about the foot-washing service. I think next year we should share some 'Minutes for Foot Washing' in worship throughout Lent and make some personal invitations for people to attend. I'll add it to the agenda for our next worship committee meeting. Goodbye and God bless!" Bob shook his head in disbelief. That truly must have been Jesus at the foot-washing service, because only the Lord could have inspired Eugenia to leave that message.

Paul had overheard. "Cool idea," he said, before popping his earbuds back in and disappearing into his room with an entire bag of chips and a jar of salsa.

Marge stood in the kitchen doorway with her hands on her hips. "Next year, I'm getting Heather to wash my feet. I don't know what she put in the water, but it must have been special to change Eugenia's heart."

Bob laughed. "Hon, I think they call it the Holy Spirit."

Marge sighed, as she often did when Bob stated the obvious. "I think I'm feeling a little of that Holy Spirit myself," she said, kicking off her shoes. She turned on the stereo, put on some Al Green, and asked Bob to dance.

17

They Took Offense

"On the sabbath he began to teach in the synagogue, and many
who heard him were astounded. They said, 'Where did this man
get all this? What is this wisdom that has been given to him?' . . .
And they took offense at him."

—MARK 6:2-3

Maybelle Howard, still wearing her coat and nervously fidgeting with
her car keys, hovered next to Bob's desk. The letter had arrived in a
plain, white envelope with no return address. There was no signature. In
fact, from reading the letter, all you could surmise about the sender was
that he or she didn't have any problems expressing their anger, and that they
weren't the best speller.

Pastor Bob pulled the letter from its nondescript envelope and read:

Dear Session Members,

How long are YOU going to let this go on? It's time to get rid of
that inbecile Pastor Bob. His latest efforts to undermine the Great
Traditions of this NOBLE Church are more rediculous than ever
before. Is NOTHING sacred around here? How long do we have
to put up with these asinine ideas? I can assure you that I speak
for a VERY LARGE contingant of this congregation when I say
he's got to go or we will. SOON! That ought to wipe the smug
smile off his stupid face.

Sincerely,

A Concerned Church Member

Bob sat back. Over the years, he had done a few things to ruffle some feathers at the church. There was the Christmas Eve when they had redesigned the service and started using a didgeridoo as part of the call to worship. There was the time he had introduced foot washing for Maundy Thursday. There was his sermon series on tithing. And when the new hymnal had been introduced, there was a near mutiny. But for the life of him, Bob couldn't think of anything he had done lately to warrant such vitriol. Although Bob had long ago accepted that an occasional poison letter was a thorn in the side of every minister, it made him feel a little sad that someone felt so angry and liked him so little. He absentmindedly drummed his fingers on the words, "A Concerned Church Member," pondering whom the author might be.

Bob shrugged and looked up at Maybelle with a weary smile. "Thanks for bringing this to my attention. I know we typically don't engage anonymous complaints, but I'd like you to add this to our agenda for the next session meeting. Please be sure to share it with the other elders." Looking a little worried, Maybelle hurried to the office to make copies.

On Tuesday evening when the session gathered, Bob lit a candle and opened the meeting with prayer. Next, he proposed that they acknowledge the elephant in the room and address the letter. He read the letter out loud, in case someone hadn't had the time to read it.

In the moments of silence that followed, there was some nervous paper shuffling around the table. Tubby Mitchell spoke first, "Bob, you know as well as we do that the church's covenant of conduct says we don't engage anonymous complaints. If someone doesn't have the bal—I mean integrity—to attach their name to their concerns, then why should we waste our time on this? I say we move on."

Jim Tinker echoed Tubby's sentiments. "Amen, Tubby. I say we toss that epistle in the circular file."

The tenderhearted Maybelle spoke next. "It hurts to read words like this. I know how hard you work for this church, Bob. I can't bear to hear you maligned in this way." There were sounds of general agreement around the table, as well as some vigorous head nodding.

Eugenia Bergstrom chimed in with, "Whoever this is, their spelling and use of capitalization is hardly a testimony to our public schools. *Inbecile*? They must mean imbecile. What in the world did you do to offend someone this time, Bob?"

This led to ten minutes of fierce debate about what had prompted such malice. By consensus, it was agreed that the recent congregational vote to choose a new carpet to replace the worn-out one in the sanctuary had driven the anonymous complainant over the edge. Bob remembered one particular ballot, with similarly lackluster spelling, that had been cast. Someone had drawn a thick, angry line through all three design choices for the new carpeting and written across the ballot in big, bold letters, "None of these are ACCEPTIBLE!"

Bob then mused out loud, "Why be mad at me? I didn't pick the colors."

Chris Nelson, the youngest elder, had been uncharacteristically quiet during the debate. Now he leaned forward, pushed his copy of the letter to the middle of the table, and slapped his hand on it, making Maybelle jump. "This isn't about Bob, folks. It's about change. It's about wanting things to be done today the way they were done thirty years ago. No offense, Bob, but it wouldn't matter who our pastor was. As long as the church welcomes new people, tries new programs, and modernizes our facility, some won't like it, and there are going to be letters like this."

Everyone chewed on this for a minute, while Chris sat back. Then, with an alarming twinkle in his eye, Chris added, "I propose we publish this."

There were gasps around the table. In the explosion of conversation that followed, Tubby and Jim warned of setting a dangerous precedent by giving voice to anonymous bullies. Eugenia wanted to know if she could first correct the spelling and capitalization. Pastor Bob said he wasn't sure how he felt about publishing something that called him an "inbecile."

Chris spoke over the cacophony, "Dudes, the newsletter goes out later this week. I say let's print it with a copy of the church's policy on sharing complaints and invite the concerned church member and his very large contingent to own their grievances. Otherwise, we are allowing ourselves to be threatened and our pastor to be bullied. I'll write the article myself. In fact, I'll make that a motion."

Eugenia seconded Chris's motion, and before you could say "inbecile," it was unanimously approved by the elders. After the vote, Bob led them all in prayer, asking God's Spirit to be at work in the church to build bridges and reconcile differences—and hoping the impending, subsequent firestorm wouldn't burn it all down.

Pastor Bob, who wasn't very good at holding onto grudges or harboring anger, had pretty much forgotten about the poison letter and the promised newsletter article by the following Monday evening, but as he sat down to dinner, there at his place at the dining room table was the newsletter, opened to Chris's article. "What's that about?" Bob's wife Marge wanted to know.

Bob slipped the newsletter onto the stack of mail on the sideboard and began to fill his plate with mashed potatoes, chicken, and salad. They shared a table grace, but Marge wasn't about to let it go. "Bob, why didn't you tell me about this? You live your life for the Lord, and this is what you get? I don't even want to think about who wrote that letter!"

Their teenage son Paul was clearly enjoying his father's discomfort. "Whoa, Dad, how dare you mess with the great traditions of this noble church?"

Bob ladled some gravy onto his mashed potatoes and liberally applied salt to everything. "Marge, you know this goes with the territory. Even Jesus offended people."

Marge scowled, but Paul, whose mouth was overly full of chicken, mashed potatoes, and salad, laughed out loud. Once he'd swallowed, Paul wisecracked, "Dad, Jesus offending people—I don't think that worked out so great for him. Do you?"

While Bob tucked into his dinner, Marge mused about shaking the dust from their feet and moving on to their next adventure—maybe a coastal call in Carolina, or how about Florida? California? Maybe the mission field! Bob cautioned, "Don't pack your bags yet, Marge. If Jesus had allowed his neighbors in Nazareth to shut him up, there'd be no gospel. I suspect that the Lord isn't finished here. Let's just see how things work out."

After dinner, the phone calls began. The first was from Charlie and Annette Miller, both on the line, like one of those holiday, family chats. They didn't mention the article, but they wanted Bob to know how much he meant to them. They reminisced about the Christmas Eve that Junior was born, their son with Down syndrome. "Jesum Crow, Bob," Charlie remembered, "When you showed up at the hospital that night to visit and pray with us, we realized we were going to be alright. What joy Junior has brought to our lives! You've been a big part of that."

No sooner had Charlie hung up than Maude Beecher phoned. In her roundabout way, Maude updated Bob on her arthritis, her garden, and her cats before getting down to business. "Bob, I don't want you getting discouraged by this complaint business. Every party has a pooper. You just got an angry one who doesn't spell very well. I've outlasted four pastors at this church. You're a good one. Keep doing the Lord's work."

It was like that all week. It wasn't just the phone calls and visits—folks showed up to tackle volunteer projects at church. Hank Tinker took Bob into the backcountry for some trout fishing.

And then there was the food. Irene Mitchell dropped off one of her rhubarb-crumb pies with a half-gallon of homemade vanilla ice cream. Lenore Claiborne came by one evening with a Crock-Pot full of her prize-winning goulash. Tommy and Kitten Stewart wined and dined Bob, Marge, and Paul at the pricey Auberge St. Moritz. That evening, as Bob surreptitiously loosened the top button of his pants under the damask tablecloth of the elegant Auberge dining table, he surmised that if the wave of pastor appreciation didn't start to ebb soon, he'd need to go on a diet.

That Sunday, despite the threat of the anonymous complainant, the church was packed, so crowded that it was impossible to guess who might be missing. The Christmas and Easter people showed up. There were new people whom Bob had never seen before. People even sat in the front pew. After church, Chris Nelson came through the line in the narthex, wearing a magenta Hawaiian shirt, cargo shorts, and hiking boots. Chris shook Bob's hand and said, "Nice sermon, Pastor Bob."

Bob smiled. "Thanks, Chris. Not bad for an inbecile, huh?"

Chris looked back at the crowded sanctuary, filled with folks smiling and visiting. "Look at that! Full house."

"Yeah," Bob answered. "Maybe I ought to offend people more often." The two men laughed. Chris wandered off to hike a mountain with his wife Nora and the kids while Bob continued to greet parishioners and visitors, hoping there might still be a few coffee–hour snacks left for him in the church hall by the time the sanctuary cleared out.

Bob never did find out who sent that letter.

18

Handed Over

"Your own nation and the chief priests have handed you
over to me. What have you done?"

—JOHN 18:35B

" I think it's time to accept the fact that she's finally dead." It was Tubby
Mitchell, sounding oddly pastoral as he flashed the beam of his flashlight into the dark expanse of the church basement, where the furnace tech
was doing his best to coax a final few days of heat out of the old boiler. From
behind the furnace, a series of clanks and muffled curses told Bob that resurrection was proving to be a challenge. Pastor Bob brushed a cobweb out of
his hair and noticed with alarm that he had managed to wipe soot across the
front of his white shirt. Maybe it was the cobwebs, but for just a moment Bob
imagined that the boiler was a giant spider, with eight asbestos-covered legs.
Bob never had cared for spiders, and he liked the prospect of buying a new
boiler and doing asbestos abatement even less.

As if reading Bob's mind, Tubby Mitchell switched off his flashlight
and shook his head. "Bob, I see a capital campaign in your future."

Bob would never know if it was the threat of a capital campaign or the
image of the giant spider that made him do it, but when the boiler suddenly
roared back to life, he gave an involuntary yell. Bob retreated to his study
while Tubby and the tech tried to hide their laughter.

Bob had just enough time to put the finishing touches on his lesson
before Bible study. They were tackling the prophet Ezekiel, whose bizarre
prophecies had left most of his class scratching their heads. Attendance was
dwindling, so in an effort to save what Bob knew to be a fast-sinking ship,

he had recruited Sharon Burke from the local theater troop to do a dramatic reading from Ezekiel, chapter thirty-four, "The Valley of the Dry Bones."

At quarter to eleven, Sharon arrived in costume. A long burlap robe wound around her body and a wooly cape shrouded her shoulders. A tall wooden staff gave her an air of prophetic authority. For good measure, she'd applied a little theatrical make-up that hollowed her cheeks and ringed her eyes, as if she'd spent long, sleepless nights listening for the word of God. This was going to be good.

And it would have been good if anyone had come. Bob and Sharon chitchatted about this and that, but after thirty minutes, they called it quits. Bob sheepishly thanked Sharon for her service to the church.

Bob popped into the office. Linda handed him a stack of pink phone messages. Juice, an Iraq war vet with PTSD, wanted to come in for a little pastoral care. Lenore Claiborne had phoned to report that the Rodriguez boy's leukemia had taken a bad turn and he was back in the hospital. Marge called, reminding him to pick up whipping cream for the pumpkin pie, which made him remember that tomorrow was Thanksgiving.

Linda cleared her throat, interrupting Bob's thoughts of Marge's pies. "You've got company, pastor." Bob looked out into the hallway where a homeless neighbor was waiting.

Pastor Bob collected his guest, who smelled of cigarettes and un-washed clothes. In fifteen years of ministry to the homeless, he had realized that, although the faces changed, the stories were often the same. A spouse's death had sent them into a tailspin. A history of incarceration had left them unemployable. A legacy of addiction had robbed them of health. A psychiatric crisis had gotten them evicted. Personal tragedy, plus hard luck, plus too few resources—all that added up to a vagabond life.

Although Pastor Bob's help was a foregone conclusion, he always took the time to welcome his homeless neighbors into his study and listen to their stories. He nodded along in sympathy and sorrow. He offered prayers that were sometimes welcomed. Bob looked at his most recent guest and felt a bit defeated. He suspected that his help might make no difference, but he offered it nonetheless. He booked his friend a room at Franco Bernard's On Belay Community on the Pliny Mill Road and sent him over to the Good News Café for a free lunch.

That got Bob thinking about his own lunch. He cruised by the Rontaks QuikMart in search of whipping cream and headed home for a sandwich. There he found Marge, prepping for tomorrow's cooking odyssey. Paul was off from school, and she had the teenager vacuuming. He moved the sweeper back and forth to the rhythm of whatever music was pulsing from the noise-cancelling headphones that Paul seemed to wear everywhere these days. Bob walked into the kitchen and tried unsuccessfully to force the whipping cream onto the top shelf of the packed fridge.

"What a nice surprise to find you at home," Bob said to Marge as she took the whipping cream and nestled it into the perfect spot on the door.

Marge looked at Bob over the top of her glasses, the way she does when he has one foot in the dog house. "Bob, don't tell me that you forgot why I'm off from work today." Bob smiled and nodded, but there was no hiding the fact that he had absolutely no idea what his wife was talking about. Marge's voice, edging half an octave higher, said, "My brother?"

Bob now remembered with a sinking feeling—Marge's brother Tony was driving up from Westchester that afternoon with his fiancée for a family Thanksgiving. Lucky for Bob, just then Marge noticed the swath of soot on the front of his white shirt and immediately forgot to give him a hard time about Tony.

"What in the world have you done to your shirt, Bob? Take that off right now while I make you a sandwich."

As Bob changed his shirt, he wondered what it was that bothered him so about Tony. It wasn't that Bob disliked his brother-in-law. He was a nice enough guy. It was more that Tony's life confronted Bob with all the things that he didn't have.

Tony earned big bucks as a financial consultant. He drove a Mercedes, sported a Rolex watch, and looked sharp in Armani suits. Tony's idea of Christmas was a ski trip to Aspen or a sailing excursion in the Caribbean.

Bob drove cars until their wheels fell off. Bob's Timex had taken a licking and kept on ticking. His clerical collars were frayed with age and too much washing. Bob's idea of vacation often involved tent camping and a tour of national parks, or a staycation in the mountains.

Pastor Bob knew that it didn't make sense, but sitting at the Thanksgiving table next to the well-groomed Tony left him feeling shabby and wishing that he could do more for his family.

Bob buttoned on his clerical collar and returned to the kitchen where Marge's ham sandwich made him forget all thoughts of shabbiness or inadequacy. As he chased his sandwich down with a glass of milk, Marge set a vase of flowers in front of him. "Take these out to Maude Beecher this afternoon, honey. Let her know how much we'll miss her tomorrow."

Back at the church, Pastor Bob visited with Juice, that vet with PTSD. Then, he headed up to the hospital to see the Rodriguez boy, who was looking and feeling much better than Lenore's message would have led Bob to believe possible. By the time he got to Sunny Vue to see Maude Beecher, the sun was low and shadows angled across the lawn. Bob parked the car, grabbed the flowers, and wandered along the long, sterile corridors in search of Maude's room.

When Bob first came to the church, he had quickly realized that Maude could be trusted for helpful guidance and sound advice. After all, she had baked the church's communion bread for more than fifty years, outlasted four pastors, and knew just about everyone in town. Maude knew where the bodies were buried—and who had buried them. Since Maude's husband and brother had died, she had often been a guest at Bob and Marge's holiday table. She came bearing bread, and often a pie or two. But earlier that year, a stroke had robbed Maude of her mobility and sent her to Sunny Vue. She wouldn't be with them this Thanksgiving.

When Bob popped his head into Maude's room, he saw touches of home: a bright granny-square afghan; a black-and-white portrait of Maude and Joe on their wedding day; the latest crayoned drawings from Maude's great-grandkids out west. As Bob turned on a lamp, put the flowers on the dresser, and sank down into a chair, Maude fixed him with bright eyes from her bed. Maude said, "It's practically Thanksgiving, Bob. You don't look very thankful." It was a neutral statement, matter of fact and nonjudgmental.

Bob smiled at his old friend, who still had the uncanny ability to read his thoughts and decipher his mood. "Want to talk about it?" she asked. Bob pushed his glasses up on his nose and looked down at his hands. Then he stared out the window, where lights had come on above the parking lot. He looked back at Maude, who raised one expectant eyebrow.

"Maude, when I handed over my life to God, I expected a lot of things—a flock to lead, the privilege of preaching the gospel, a chance to serve the community, the opportunity to pray with and for folks—but I didn't know how hard it would feel some days. I never anticipated the sleepless nights, worrying about raising money to fix a boiler or balance the budget. I never knew how lonely I would feel when no one shows up for my programs. I never thought about how much my family would be expected to sacrifice. I never imagined how powerless I would be to heal sick bodies or comfort grieving people or calm unsettled minds. I'm not complaining, Maude, but some days I wish it wasn't quite so hard." Maude nodded, and the two sat in silence.

When Maude spoke at last, it was with that same tone she had used when Bob first came to the church and needed help navigating a pastoral slump. "Sounds to me like you need to do some more handing over, Bob."

Bob's blank stare prompted her to go on. "Bob, as a young man you may have made some big decision to hand your life over to God, but it doesn't sound like you've handed over your ministry. Who do you think you are? Jesus? Next, you'll be complaining that you can't walk on water, or multiply loaves and fish to stop world hunger."

Bob's mouth dropped open and his brow creased as he tried to decide if he should laugh or be offended.

In the end, Maude made the decision for him, smiling a lopsided grin and waving him over to her bedside. "You're gonna be just fine, Bob. Now give me a hug and get home to Marge before your dinner gets cold."

As Bob drove across town, he saw the moon, hanging like an orange sickle low in the night sky. Here and there, stars began to glow in the growing darkness. Maybe Maude was right. Maybe he needed to hand it all over—the boiler, the capital campaign, the Bible study, his homeless friends, his family, his meager finances, his ailing parishioners. Bob pulled into the driveway behind Tony's Mercedes. Maybe, just maybe, in all his inadequacy he was going to be okay, Bob thought, because he wasn't really in it alone. He was in it with the Lord. Jesus hadn't promised his friends that it would be easy, but he had promised them that he would be with them until the end of the age.

Bob turned off the car and sat for just a moment, feeling oddly light and a little giddy. He felt like a kid on his first day of school. He felt like a minor league player called up to the big leagues. He felt like a master mariner cresting a wave on a limitless horizon. He felt like a big piece of Marge's pumpkin pie, slathered with extra whipped cream.

19

Restored

"Restore us, O God of hosts; let your face shine, that we may be saved."

—PSALM 80: 7

"Look, the virgin shall conceive and bear a son, and they shall name him Emmanuel, which means, 'God is with us.'"

—MATTHEW 1:23

The front door opened and softly closed. "Bruce, is that you?" Jenny called from the kitchen. She was putting the finishing touches on Christmas cookies, piping royal icing onto gingerbread men and Bethlehem stars. Jenny listened while her son moved through the house, checking closets, looking under beds, pulling back the shower curtain, climbing the attic stairs. Bruce had been that way ever since he had returned from the Middle East after four long tours of duty.

Bruce, with his friends Todd and Franco, had joined up right out of high school, enlisting midway through their senior year, eager to serve their nation. Jenny hadn't been happy about it. At the time, Bruce was passing up a promising opportunity to train for Olympic speed skating. From the time he could barely walk, Bruce had been bombing around the ice on skates. A coach had seen the boy's potential and channeled all that young energy into a successful junior career on the short track. It had culminated with a big win at the state games. That's where the nickname Juice took hold. In long, low tones, fans chanted, "Bruce the Juice! Bruce the Juice! Bruce the Juice!" as he skated to victory after victory.

No amount of persuading would have changed Bruce's mind about the Marine Corps, so Jenny made the best of it. She baked most weeks and shipped out cookies that took three months to arrive at the base. She had her third-grade class draw pictures and write notes for the men and women with whom Bruce served. They Skyped whenever they had the chance. Jenny listened with fear as Bruce described patrols in 130-degree heat, roadside bombs, and door-to-door hunts for insurgents. Jenny knew there were worse things, too—things that Bruce wouldn't discuss.

Jenny considered herself lucky when Bruce came home for good. Her friends Tubby and Irene Mitchell had not been so fortunate with their son Todd, one of Bruce's best friends. Todd was killed early in their first tour. Their other high school friend, Franco, had spent time as a prisoner of war. As Jenny stood on the airport tarmac and watched Bruce walk over to her, so handsome in his uniform, she had wept tears of joy, thankful that the ordeal was over.

Later, Jenny realized that her ordeal was just beginning. It started with the patrols, like what Bruce was doing then—walking through the house, scanning for danger, making sure she was safe. Bruce was hypervigilant and sensitive. He saw threats and dangers where none existed. He'd lost his easygoing nature and had a short fuse that could be set off by an unexpected loud noise, or a raucous crowd at a hockey game, or, especially, fireworks.

Worst of all were the nightmares that kept him edgy and sleep-deprived. Bruce began drinking. On the night Jenny found Bruce unconscious on the bathroom floor with an empty fifth of Scotch and a bottle of pills, she realized that her son was suicidal. She had to admit that, although the tour of duty was over for Bruce, her son had never really come home.

If it hadn't been for the church, Jenny wasn't sure what would have happened. She confided in her friends, the Mitchells. Although Todd hadn't come back from Iraq, Tubby and Irene had welcomed Bruce home like the son they had lost. After the bathroom incident, Jenny called them up. Tubby and Irene came over to the house. They listened with love and patience. Then, with humility and tears, they had bowed their heads together and prayed for help.

Jenny shouldn't have been surprised when Pastor Bob showed up early the next morning. When she opened the front door and saw him on her doorstep, looking rumpled and gray, Jenny burst into tears. Bob came right in, sat her down, took her hand, and listened. When she finished, he shared one of his little smiles and gave her hand an encouraging squeeze.

"I have hope for Bruce," he said. "The Lord is going to help us all through this. Let's trust him."

With Bob's help, Jenny had reached out to the VA. One of Bruce's former commanding officers convinced him to try an in-patient treatment program. There, Bruce learned that he suffered from PTSD, and he was able to stop drinking. When Bruce came back to the village, his friend Franco got him involved with a veterans' support group that met weekly to share about their experiences in a safe, supportive environment.

The last three years, things had been better. Bruce had gotten a job at the sawmill. He liked wearing the over-sized, hearing-protection headphones, driving the forklift, loading logs into the bandsaw, and stacking boards. He had a natural gift for looking at a tree and seeing the best way to cut it, a skill that rivaled the high-tech computer models that they use these days.

Even better, Bruce reconnected with his former coach and was back on long blades. He helped out with coaching the high school team and trained faithfully at the rink and gym. When Jenny saw her son in his skate suit, back on the ice, she saw the ghost of the boy he had been, before he had gone to the Middle East.

In time, Bruce's veterans group became a band of brothers whom he could turn to for help. Lately, Bruce had even taken to volunteering. On most Saturdays, you could find him down at the Good News Café, helping Tubby Mitchell serve hot food to hard-luck neighbors.

Bruce still checked the house every time he came home. He still had nightmares. Jenny would awaken in the middle of the night with her heart pounding as Bruce in his bedroom down the hall screamed, "Incoming!" or "Take cover!" or, hardest of all to hear, "Todd, watch out! O, my God! No!"

Jenny filled a cup with coffee, got out a plate, and loaded it with cookies. She listened while Bruce took off his coat in the entry. She smiled as he stood in the doorway to the kitchen, scanning the room for danger. "All clear?" she asked.

Bruce relaxed a bit. He smiled at his mother, grabbed a gingerbread man, and bit its head off, "All clear, Ma. Thanks for the cookies."

The two sat at the table and visited. Jenny shared the latest achievements of her third–graders and Bruce talked about his day at the mill. Then, Bruce rummaged through the fridge for leftovers while Jenny wiped down the counters and prepared to head up to bed. "Don't forget that tomorrow is Christmas Eve, Bruce. We've got the candlelight service at seven o'clock. See if you can knock off work in time to get a quick shower before the service. I'll meet you at church."

Now, the Presbyterian Church was one of the few places where Bruce felt truly safe. He knew every inch of the building from playing endless rounds of sardines there as a child with Franco and Todd. From the narthex, Bruce scanned the coat room and the sanctuary before the candlelight service. Pastor Bob bid him a hasty "Merry Christmas" as he rushed by in search of batteries for his cordless microphone. Tubby Mitchell gave Bruce a friendly nod of welcome from the choir, up on the chancel.

Bruce's friend Franco greeted him with a handshake and pulled him in for a hug. "Juice! Merry Christmas, bro." They settled into the pew next to Jenny and waited for the service to begin.

It was warm in the darkened sanctuary. Candlelight glowed from the Lord's Table and the Advent wreath. One by one, readers shared in measured tones scripture's story of human sin and God's salvation. The gentle swell of favorite carols flowed like a gentle ocean, cradling Bruce in familiar sound. His eyes grew heavy, his chin dropped to his chest, and Bruce fell asleep, right there in the third pew from the back.

He was standing on a frozen lake. All around, trees were covered with snow, and his breath hung in clouds before his face. Someone had carefully laid out a skating oval, slick with fresh ice. Bruce looked down. He was wearing his skate suit and his feet were shod with familiar long blades. On the far side of the oval, two Marines were skating, taking their time, talking and laughing together. Bruce pulled up his hood, crouched in a starter's stance, and took off. His left arm was aerodynamically tucked up behind. His right arm swung to the cadence of his feet. His heart filled with the joy of movement.

It didn't take long to catch up with the other two skaters. Bruce slowed to a stop with a showy spray of ice, and the two Marines turned around. Bruce looked into a face that he knew just as well as his own. He had played with him for countless hours as a child. He had seen him die in a thousand nightmares. It was Todd Mitchell. Todd! He was perfect. In fact, he looked absolutely luminous, filled with light and joy and laughter.

"Ah, Bruce the Juice," Todd greeted him, "You still got it, brother! So glad you could make it. We've been waiting for you for such a long time."

Bruce hugged his friend Todd so hard that they almost fell over. Finally, Todd thumped him on the back and gave him a little push away, saying, "Hey, Bruce, this is my friend, Emmanuel. You're gonna love him."

And with that, Bruce woke up. It may have been the vestiges of his dream, but the whole sanctuary gleamed softly with a gentle light that seemed to emerge from the very substance of pews and pulpit, chancel and cross. The face of every worshiper shone as they held aloft candles and joined the choir in singing "Silent Night, Holy Night." Jenny reached over and held her son's hand, whispering, "Are you alright, Bruce?"

Bruce scanned the sanctuary. He felt strange. He felt something that he hadn't felt in years, hadn't felt since before his time in the Middle East. If he had to put a name to it, he might even have said it was peace. Bruce smiled at his mother, "I'm fine, Ma. I *really* am fine."

Years later, when Jenny MacLeod talked about that Christmas, she said it was the year that her son Bruce finally came home from war.

20

A Lamp Shining in a Dark Place

"You will do well to be attentive to this as to a lamp shining in a dark place, until the day dawns and the morning star rises in your hearts."

—2 PETER 1:19B

Chris Nelson stepped inside the door of the Bluebird Diner and stomped the snow off his boots. As Chris waved and approached the table, Pastor Bob saw a neon Hawaiian shirt peeking out from under Chris's parka, and when Chris pulled off his hat, Bob saw the familiar shaved head and pierced ears. But as Betty Lou Campbell waited to take their orders, Bob noticed Chris tugging at his goatee, the way he did when the session had an important decision to make, or one of his kids was sick, or he had a big deadline at work. In fact, as Bob looked a little closer, he wondered, could those be a few first, grey hairs in Chris's beard?

While the men sipped coffee and waited for their food, Bob asked, "Chris, how are you doing? You look like you are shouldering a heavy burden these days."

The younger man's eyebrows shot up and he peered at Bob over the top of his wire-rimmed glasses. Bob gave Chris a little encouraging nod, like he does when he's trying to get the kids to share during children's time. Chris responded, "Wow! Where do I start?"

As they lunched on burgers, fries, and pie, Bob listened. Chris's mom was sick. She'd been feeling tired and had lost weight. Lots of tests had yielded a diagnosis of lymphoma. Although her prognosis was good, chemo and radiation loomed ahead. Until they got to the other side of treatment, Chris's mom would be moving into the guest room. The timing wasn't great, because Chris's wife Nora had just gone back to work after maternity leave.

Their two older kids were awesome, but incredibly busy with dance lessons and skating and piano. Chris felt that, between work, school, day care, doctor's appointments, session meetings, and extracurricular activities, just figuring out the logistics of who needed to be where at what time was proving to be a nightmare of epic proportions.

On top of all that was Chris's work as a journalist and editor at the local newspaper. "Have you seen the news lately, Bob?" Chris wanted to know. "It's not good out there. I'm tired of reporting about school shootings and war in the Middle East and the toxic political climate in Washington." Bob nodded in commiseration and forked in a big bite of cherry pie to ward off the evil specter of national politics.

Chris continued, "I think my days at the paper could be numbered, Bob. Print media is going the way of the dinosaur. I should be down in New York or Washington, hustling for freelance assignments with major news outlets, not plugging away at the *Little City News*." Bob noted with some alarm that Chris's eyes had taken on a hunted look, the kind of look that Bob himself wore as the liturgical calendar lurched into Holy Week, when he had more worship to plan and pastoral responsibilities to fulfill than were humanly possible.

After Betty Lou cleared away the dishes and refilled the coffee, Bob cleared his throat. "Chris, it sounds like you could use a lamp to shine in that dark place."

Chris looked a little puzzled. He could think of many things he could use—a nanny, a medical miracle, a new job, a clone—but not one of those things was a lamp.

Bob hurried to explain. "The Apostle Peter, when he faced tough times, remembered the day that Jesus took him up on the mountain, the day he saw Jesus transfigured. That memory of Christ in glory, those words God spoke from heaven—they reminded Peter that he was part of something holy, that the future was in God's hands." Bob's attempt to explain seemed to only bewilder Chris more, so he kept going.

"Chris, did I ever tell you the story of when Paul was born?" Chris shook his head.

"Well, Marge was so sick during the pregnancy and had such a difficult delivery that we knew Paul was it. We were fine with having an only child. Yet, when I sat in the hospital room and held my newborn son, I felt terrified. Paul was so perfect, and I was so sure that I was going to mess things up. I'd lost my father when I was young. Who would teach me? And you know what they say about preacher's kids. How could I pastor a church and be a father? Everyone rejoiced over Paul's birth, but my smile hid a world of fear and uncertainty. I was sure I would fail." Bob remembered and paused, with a faraway look, and took a sip of coffee.

"But then I had one of those bright and shining moments," Bob smiled.

Chris looked skeptical. "You saw Jesus transfigured?"

This made Bob laugh and choke a little on his coffee. "I wish. No, not exactly, Chris," Bob answered while he dabbed at his shirt with a napkin. "One Sunday morning, we had Paul baptized. As we stood at the baptismal font and cradled Paul, I remembered that Paul wasn't just our child. Paul was God's beloved child. Then, in the liturgy when the whole congregation affirmed that they would nurture Paul in the faith, I realized that Paul belonged to them, too. In parenting, I would sometimes make a mess of things—something that Paul likes to point out now that he is in high school—but Marge and I wouldn't be undertaking that big job alone. God would be with us, and so would the church. I stopped being afraid of being a parent, and I started to love it. That was my lamp in a dark place. Whenever I'm ready to throw in the towel with being a dad, I remember that moment, and I find the grace to be a better father."

Now Chris was nodding. "I like that, Bob. The lamp shining—it's the memory that gets you through, the moment that gives you hope. I'll see if I can come up with a few lamps of my own." Bob picked up the check and the two men stood up, shook hands, shrugged back into their coats, and left.

Chris pulled his cap down and walked back to the newspaper. The village always looked magical with a blanket of snow. The mountains, deep with powder, were bright in the afternoon sun—not quite transfigured, but nice all the same. Back at the office, Chris remembered the day he had landed the job at the paper as a newly graduated journalist. He'd gotten the job over more seasoned reporters because the publisher believed Chris had the unconventional perspective and grit to do something special. When Chris had heard the news, he had known he'd found what God wanted him to do with his life, and where he was supposed to do it. It had been one of those bright and shining moments.

Later, when Chris got home from work, Nora greeted him at the door. She had their infant slung on her hip. Something that looked like squash was mashed in her hair. Her cheeks were flushed from cooking in the warm kitchen, and she smelled good—like squash and baby wipes and roasted chicken. Chris remembered the day he had asked Nora to marry him.

They'd climbed to the top of Garnet Mountain's fire tower. There, with the canoe wilderness stretching as far as the eye could see, Chris had gotten down on a knee and popped the question. Nora had said, "Yes," all matter of fact, like she'd been waiting months for him to figure out just how blessed he was. It was one of those bright and shining moments.

After dinner, Chris did the dishes while Nora tackled baths. Then, Chris got the older kids settled into bed with five pages of Harry Potter apiece. Back downstairs, Chris and Nora sat on the couch and clicked on the TV. Within moments, Nora's head began to nod, and although Chris would never tell her, she snored. Over in the corner of the family room, Chris spotted something wooden, slender, tall, and primal looking. Chris walked across the room and smiled. "Didgeridoo!" he said softly, fitting the aboriginal wind instrument to his mouth and blowing until an eerie moan escaped.

Nora sprang to life. "Chris, unless *you* want to get the baby back to sleep, I suggest you leave the didgeridoo alone." But Chris was on the move now. With his coat on, the didgeridoo clamped under his arm, and the car keys in his hand, he headed for the door. "Babe, I'll be back in twenty minutes."

As Chris drove through the village, he remembered the first Christmas Eve that he had played his didgeridoo at church. When the service had begun, the lights dimmed and the sanctuary grew quiet. Chris had taken a deep breath and begun to puff and blow into his didgeridoo, and its strange, primordial, droning call leapt forth into the darkness, like the breath from God that had hovered above the waters of chaos before creation. While the sound of the didgeridoo faded away, a single spotlight had caught a silvery and golden star, shining down from the top of the nave. Although Chris had attended Christmas Eve services from the time he was tiny, in the cry of the didgeridoo and the glow of the star, Chris had sensed for the first time God's ancient love for the world, a holy heartbeat echoing across all time and space. It had been a bright and shining moment.

Chris parked in front of Pastor Bob's house. It must have been close to zero degrees out. His breath hung in icy clouds and the moon had a luminous halo. Even though it was late and the house was dark, Chris got out of the car. He walked through the snow, his boots squeaking in the cold, until he stood in the middle of the yard. He fit the didgeridoo to his mouth and began to play. Deep rumbling sighs and barks erupted from the instrument into the dark winter night. Up and down the street, dogs barked and lights began to come on. Pastor Bob's front door opened and

Bob stood on the porch, disheveled and shivering in his robe and slippers. "Chris? What's up?"

Chris smiled. "The lamp is shining in those dark places, Bob. The lamp is shining." Chris played a little more, then got back into the car and drove home, feeling strangely light and filled with hope.

21

Prepare the Way

"Prepare the way of the Lord, make his paths straight."

—MARK 1:3B

No one loved getting ready for Christmas more than Dermott Campbell. Every year on Black Friday, when most folks were out shopping for Christmas gifts, Dermott would rise early while the sun was just a dim pink glow behind the mountains. He'd pull on his insulated coveralls, thickest wool socks, and warmest cap. Then he'd head out back to the garage to begin his preparations.

For more years than people could remember, Dermott had won the village Christmas Spirit Award for his holiday decorations. But this year, Dermott knew he would face some serious competition. Rumor had it that Dermott's young neighbor Archie Leonard was working on a "Hundred Acre Wood" theme, complete with giant blow-up figures of Tigger, Winnie-the-Pooh, and Piglet dancing around a twenty-foot-tall Christmas tree to the tune of "God Rest Ye Merry Gentlemen." Dermott had even heard that Archie's wife had stitched up a fleecy Eeyore costume for their Newfoundland, as well as woolly Kanga and Roo suits with Santa caps to fit herself and their toddler. Archie was reportedly working on his own Christopher Robin outfit. How could anyone top that?

When it came to his Christmas decorations, Dermott was a traditionalist; none of this New Age, Disney stuff for him. And after all these years, Dermott had his yard preparations down to a science. First, he would hang the green, artificial wreaths with their cheery, red bows, one for every window of the house. Then, he would place an electric candle on each sill to lend some colonial charm. Next, Dermott would spend days working on the outdoor lights—icicle strings hanging from the eves, multi-colored flashers strung around doors and windows, and nets of warm amber lights draped over all the shrubs. After the greens and lights were up, Dermott would tackle the nativity scene, a cozy, hay-filled lean-to for a stable that sheltered life-size, papier-mâché figures of Mary, Joseph, a couple of shepherds, and the three Magi with their gifts. There were even some plastic camels that Dermott liked to place in strategic locations across the lawn, as if they were taking a well-deserved rest after a long caravan.

This year, in response to the challenge of Archie Leonard's "Hundred Acre Wood" tableau, Dermott had decided to give his holiday decorations an interfaith appeal, and so he had crafted a giant, wooden, musical menorah with nine beautiful points of electric-candle light. He planned to light a new candle for each night of Hanukkah. Dermott had wired the menorah to a Clapper, so that when he clapped on, the lively strains of "*Ma'oz Tzur*" would break forth for all to hear. Take that, Archie Leonard!

The crowning achievement, though, of Dermott's Christmas décor was the sleigh and eight reindeer mounted on the roof of his house. For years, Dermott had combed yard sales for taxidermy pieces, at last managing to come up with the stuffed heads of five deer, a moose, an elk, and a llama. He had wired the heads to burlap-covered armatures, and if you squinted your eyes just right in the winter darkness, they looked *exactly* like Santa's reindeer. Dermott had even replaced the nose of the lead deer with a neon-bright, red light, just like Rudolph's. For the final touch, Dermott wired up high-powered spotlights to properly illuminate his holiday handiwork.

Every night of Christmas week, Dermott would strip off the coveralls and bundle his skinny body into a huge, well-padded, overstuffed Santa suit. Then, he would climb up onto the roof and take a seat in Santa's sleigh. For hours on end, he would shout, "Ho, ho, ho! Merry Christmas!" while throwing hard candies down to the neighborhood children who came to gaze in fear and wonder at the awesome sight.

Dermott's wife Betty Lou, who was a deacon at the Presbyterian Church, had long ago resigned herself to the fact that she and Dermott had very different ways of preparing for Christmas. But she couldn't help hoping that someday her husband might take a more spiritual and less electrical approach to the holiday. As Dermott hung wreaths, she'd call out, "Dermott, why don't you come down here and help me load this cranberry jelly into the car for the Good News Café?" Or, as Dermott untangled strings of lights, Betty Lou would suggest, "Sweetie, why don't you come shopping with me? We have to pick out a little boy's toy for the Holiday Helpers."

But Dermott was always reluctant to leave his preparations. "Aw, Betty Lou, can't you see I'm busy? You know I need every spare minute I can find if I'm gonna win the Christmas Spirit Award. You think Archie Leonard is out shopping right now? I don't think so."

Betty Lou would sigh and go about her good works. "Okay, Dermott, maybe next year."

One Saturday afternoon, Pastor Bob stopped by the house. Dermott had the lean-to up and was carefully nestling his delicate papier-mâché Mary and Joseph into the straw next to the manger. "Dermott!" Pastor Bob called out, "I see you're getting ready to win that Christmas Spirit Award again. What an extraordinary nativity scene!"

Dermott's broad smile lit up his face like the Bethlehem star. He stepped back to admire his work. "You think this is something, just wait, Pastor Bob!"

Before Pastor Bob could respond, Dermott had run back to the garage, like a man on a mission. He returned a few moments later with a Cabbage Patch doll swaddled in yard upon yard of translucent, silver, lamé fabric. Dermott had clearly been raiding Betty Lou's fabric stash. "There!" Dermott said, thrusting the doll into Pastor Bob's arms.

Pastor Bob looked from the doll to Dermott with a puzzled look until Dermott shook his head with impatience and said, "Pastor Bob, it's the baby Jesus!"

"Oh! Oh!" Pastor Bob said, holding the doll out at arm's length to get a better look. It was the closest that Pastor Bob had ever come to being speechless, but he soon recovered. "Dermott, I need some strong arms to load holiday-food boxes over at the armory. I was hoping you could come and help out."

Dermott looked from Pastor Bob to the baby Jesus, still waiting to be placed in the manger. "Well, Pastor Bob, I'm kinda busy here. It *is* the baby Jesus, you know."

Pastor Bob handed the Cabbage Patch doll back to Dermott and shrugged his shoulders. "Maybe next year, Dermott."

"Yeah, sure. Next year, Bob," Dermott answered, already turning back to his work.

The Friday before Christmas, Dermott finished his preparations. As he stood back and looked at his handiwork, a tear came to his eye. It was his best effort yet. Betty Lou came out, bundled in her warmest winter coat, and surveyed his work. "Goodness, Dermott, you have outdone yourself this year. Just beautiful! I'm off to do some caroling with the church. We're visiting our homebound friends. Why don't you come, dear? You'll love it."

But Dermott only shook his head. "Betty Lou, I'm still busy here. I think I've got a few lights to tweak. You go on, and have yourself a good time."

Betty Lou wasn't the only one to turn up to admire Dermott's work. While Dermott was testing out his Clapper-driven menorah, who should appear but young Archie Leonard? He was standing out at the curb with his mouth wide open in awe. "Dermott, you're my hero! How do you do it every year? It's just amazing!"

Dermott felt himself warming up to his young neighbor. "Well, Archie," he said, "just give yourself a few more years and they'll be giving you the Christmas Spirit Award. Just wait."

Archie looked hopeful and humbled, all at the same time. "Say, Dermott, I'm wondering if you can help me. I'm having a tough time keeping my inflatable Winnie-the-Pooh under control. He's got that big Pooh belly, and every time a good wind comes along, I'm afraid he's going to sail away. I could really use your expertise."

Dermott looked at his younger neighbor with irritation. "Archie, can't you see I'm busy here? Get some coated cable and lash your Pooh to Tigger and Piglet, then tie 'em all down good. You gotta learn from experience, son. That's what I did." Dermott stalked off to adjust the spotlight on the baby Jesus, leaving Archie to fend for himself.

As dusk fell on December twenty-third, the Christmas Spirit Award judges were scheduled to tour the town and make their decision, so Dermott bundled himself into his overstuffed Santa suit and prepared to head up on the roof.

"Dermott!" Betty Lou stopped him. "Surely, you're not going up on that roof in this weather!"

Dermott looked out the picture window. Snow was falling fast, and a nasty, gusty breeze was picking up, whipping white veils across the yard that obscured the view. "Oh, no!" Dermott groaned.

Betty Lou put a hand on the sleeve of his red, velvet suit, saying, "Honey, why don't you come down to church with me? Pastor Bob is leading some kind of special prayer program to help us prepare for the coming of Christmas."

Dermott just stared at his wife. "Betty Lou," he said angrily, gesturing to the lights and ornaments out on the lawn, "I've just spent a whole month preparing for Christmas. I don't think I need Pastor Bob to tell me how to do that." With that, Dermott marched off to the roof, and Betty Lou got into the car and drove to church.

Dermott sat in Santa's sleigh high above the yard, watching as the snow grew heavier. He felt the wind tugging at his fur-trimmed hat. He watched as his reindeer swayed dangerously in their traces with each gust. Dermott clapped on his musical menorah, but he didn't feel much like singing along, and he certainly didn't want to shout out, "Ho! Ho! Ho! Merry Christmas!" He regretted his harsh words to Betty Lou. For a moment, as he looked down at all the lights and decorations twinkling in the falling snow, a small cloud of doubt obscured his thoughts. Maybe Betty Lou was right. Maybe preparing for Christmas was supposed to be more about prayer, and caring, and helping neighbors, and less about holiday decorations and the Christmas Spirit Award. Dermott looked over at the baby Jesus, nestled in the straw-filled manger, and called out, "What about it, baby Jesus? Have I got this Christmas spirit thing all wrong?"

Dermott felt himself to be on the verge of some deep knowing when his thoughts were rudely interrupted by young Archie Leonard. There he was at the edge of the yard, dressed up like Christopher Robin in his Mary Janes, jumping up and down, yelling, and pointing down the street into the darkness. Dermott clapped off his musical menorah and stood up to try to listen, but by now it was so windy that all he could hear was something like "OAGOOON!"

"Speak up there, Archie!" Dermott shouted above the rising wind.

Archie only jumped up and down all the more, looking panicked and gesturing wildly into the snowy darkness. "OAGOOON!"

Dermott turned around and peered into the night sky. His ears were the first to notice something, the tinkling of Christmas music—an old English hymn, "God Rest Ye Merry Gentlemen." As Dermott strained to see in the darkness, three dim shapes emerged—big shapes, yellow and orange and soft pink—flying high on the strengthening gale, directly toward him. Suddenly, Archie's crazy yell made sense. "Rogue balloon!"

Before Dermott knew it, Winnie-the-Pooh, Tigger, and Piglet were upon him and had swept him off his feet. For a moment, he felt like he was flying, dancing high above the ground with his friends from the Hundred Acre Wood, but it didn't last long. Pooh, Tigger, and Piglet swooped off into the darkness while Dermott plummeted earthward, landing spread-eagle on top of the lean-to. The last thing he saw before losing consciousness was the baby Jesus, floating on a silvery cloud and smiling down on the chaos below.

When Betty Lou got home from church later, it looked like a bomb had gone off in the front yard. The lean-to had collapsed under the force of Dermott's impact. The papier-mâché figures within had been smashed to pieces. The yard was littered with straw and body parts, poking up out of the snow. One of the Magi's heads was speared upon the musical menorah, and the torso of the Virgin Mary had shot right through the picture window and into the house. Only the baby Jesus had survived unscathed, tossed improbably high into the air before coming to rest in the crook of the maple tree, where the wind made his legs appear to kick with childish delight, as if he were having a good laugh at the demise of all Dermott's handiwork.

Dermott and Archie Leonard stood there, glumly surveying the wreckage. Dermott's Santa suit looked as if it had been deflated. Wads of dense, white stuffing were popping out of every seam.

"O, my Lord! Dermott?" Betty Lou called out. "Are you okay?"

Dermott smiled and gave a little wave. "I'm alright, Betty Lou. My Santa suit saved me."

Archie, looking shell-shocked, could only mutter, "Rogue balloon."

"Why don't you men come inside and tell me all about it?" Betty Lou invited. They picked their way across the snow, careful to avoid the carnage, and went in. While Betty Lou made hot chocolate, Dermott and Archie told their story. About midway through, Kanga, Roo, and Eeyore showed up in search of Christopher Robin, and Archie went home to assess his own damage.

"Betty Lou," Dermott said as they looked through their broken picture window at the big mess outside.

"Yes, dear," she answered.

"I think I learned something tonight, Betty Lou."

"What's that, honey?"

"Well, it's about the Christmas spirit and preparing the way of the Lord."

"Hmm?"

"Well, next year, Betty Lou, don't let me tell you that I'm too busy to help and to serve and to pray."

"But Dermott, what about your Christmas Spirit Award?"

"I'm thinking it's time to move on, Betty Lou. Let Archie Leonard have a crack at it. Maybe I can even help him. Lord knows, the man doesn't know how to tie down a balloon."

As the snow fell, the baby Jesus happily kicked in the crook of the maple tree; Tigger, Winnie-the-Pooh, and Piglet adventured off into the night; and Dermott and Betty Lou boarded up the picture window and went to bed.

22

The Gift of Peace

"Peace I leave with you; my peace I give to you. I do not give to you
as the world gives. Do not let your hearts be troubled, and do not
let them be afraid."

—JOHN 14:27

Somewhere on the hill above the house, a litter of coyote pups was trying out their first yips. The sugar maple in the backyard creaked in the
stiffening breeze, sending a cascade of seeds on a whirling journey past the
bedroom window. Downstairs in the fridge, the icemaker dumped a fresh
batch of cubes into the plastic bin. Pastor Bob rolled over and pushed the
little button on the top of his alarm clock. For just a second, the bright, digital, clock face lit up—2:13 a.m. Pastor Bob sighed. He couldn't remember
the last time he'd had a good night's sleep.

It wasn't that Bob wasn't tired. His calendar was hopelessly overcrowd-
ed, and he was long overdue for a vacation. Most days, he was on the go, from
early morning Bible studies to lunchtime counseling sessions to after-dinner
committee meetings. But at the end of the day when Bob's head hit the pillow,
sleep eluded him. Instead, all the busyness and chaos of his day seemed to rise
up to meet him in ways that were decidedly not restful.

He could see Maybelle Howard, slowly pushing her walker down
the medical-center hallway with a careworn expression on her face. It was
Maybelle's second hip-replacement surgery. Although she'd bounced right
back after the first, this second procedure seemed a whole lot more pain-
ful. That afternoon, worried that their mom just wasn't up to living alone
anymore, Maybelle's kids had, with a measure of hopefulness, dropped off

some glossy brochures from the local assisted-living center. They showed spry, silver-haired elders relaxing by a roaring fire or tending a flower garden or laughing at some shared jest around the dinner table. Bob thought it looked kind of nice, but as he paced the hall with Maybelle, she grimly said she'd sooner die than go to assisted living.

Maybelle's mobility troubles got Bob thinking about Molly Hall. It seemed like only yesterday that Molly had set a new standard for confirmation service projects by organizing a church work crew to go down to New Jersey for disaster relief after Hurricane Sandy had devastated the shoreline. Molly had been the kind of bright and passionate kid who made you feel hopeful about "today's youth." But in her freshman year of college, the car Molly was riding in was broadsided by a drunk driver. Molly had suffered a traumatic brain injury and broken pelvis. Over the past few years, Molly had been through repeated rounds of orthopedic surgery, followed by rigorous physical, occupational, and speech therapy, and more, but it was clear she would never return to school. It had been a long, slow road to healing, with stops along the way in the dark land of depression and despair. The last time they had visited, though, Molly had announced with great pride that she would be on the church's Hurricane Maria work crew, bound for Puerto Rico in just a few weeks.

Of course, Bob would be on the work crew, too, if he survived the Ladies Auxiliary Annual Chicken Barbecue, scheduled for the coming weekend. Every corner of the church kitchen overflowed with Hank Tinker's secret barbecue sauce, heads of cabbage ready to be chopped for coleslaw, ears of corn waiting to be shucked, and countless bags of brown-n-serve dinner rolls. The freezer was jam-packed with cartons of ice cream to top the berry cobbler. Just that afternoon, the church's thirty-year-old, industrial-sized refrigerator had succumbed to all the excitement, heaving a dying growl and leaving a large, unfortunate puddle across the entire kitchen floor. After he finished mopping up, Bob had been able to order a replacement fridge, but it wouldn't be delivered until the morning. The ladies had all been sent home with big boxes of chicken and cartons of ice cream to tend overnight. How in the world they would be able to pull off the barbecue without the organizational powers of Heather Rodriguez, who was home on bed rest while expecting twins, was a mystery that Bob didn't dare to fathom.

Bob sighed and pushed the little button on top of his clock again. In the soft electric glow, Bob could make out 2:15 a.m. How could only two minutes have passed when it felt like an eternity? Bob rolled over and looked at Marge, who had always had the coveted, if annoying, gift of untroubled sleep. She had one arm thrown across her eyes, and her chest rose and fell in deep, slow, even breaths. Her eyelids fluttered with untold dreams. She looked young in the moonlight. She definitely didn't look like someone who spent half the night worrying about this, that, and the other thing.

That got Bob thinking about his honey-do list. Marge had wanted him to put a new seal on the leaky downstairs toilet for months now. And her latest remodeling plans called for Bob to paint the guest bedroom puce, even though Bob had no idea what the color puce might actually look like. He really did need to make a dump run because, as Marge liked to tell him with an ironic grin, their garbage cans "stinketh." Sometime this summer, he would need to take Paul to look at colleges, even though Bob's stomach tied up in nervous knots every time he thought about the cost of college tuition. Then, for the 934th time, Bob wondered if he would ever be able to retire. It wasn't looking good.

That was enough to make Bob sit up and swing his legs over the edge of the bed. He debated whether to go to the kitchen and drink some cold milk right out of the carton or take the dog for a walk. As if on cue, Sparky's tail began to thump, and the big yellow lab rose to put two feet up on the bed in hopeful anticipation. This was enough to make Marge groan, so Bob ventured a hopeful, "Honey? You awake?" Marge's answer sounded somewhere between a "no" and an "oh," so Bob ventured on. "Marge, I can't sleep."

Marge rolled over and looked at Bob. He'd gotten a lot of gray hair this past year, as if middle age had decided to pounce on him all of a sudden. Marge reached over and placed a comforting hand on Bob's shoulder. "Bob," she said with the same patient tone that she had used with Paul when he was a little boy, "don't you think you'd be better off talking to the Lord about that than talking to me?" Marge gave him a little smile and turned away. By the sound of her breathing, she was asleep again within about thirty seconds. Darn you, Marge.

Bob pushed the hopeful Sparky down off the bed and stretched out. Bob turned his thoughts to Jesus and, as Jesus often did when Bob thought about him, Jesus was right there with him. Jesus's face wore the same sort of interested and caring expression that Bob's face wore when one of his parishioners knocked on his door with a heavy burden.

"Lord," Bob prayed, "I can't sleep."

Jesus nodded as if this made perfect sense. "Ah" he said, "Ladies Auxiliary Annual Chicken Barbecue?"

Bob instantly began to wonder why in the world he hadn't thought of talking to the Lord earlier. "Lord," Bob said, "you don't know the half of it." And before Bob knew it, he had told Jesus about all those worries and troubles and pastoral cares that seemed to march across the screen of his mind nightly, like some unwanted, unending movie.

When Bob had finished, Jesus nodded and said, "I've got exactly what you need, Bob. Peace." Just the way Jesus said the word—"Peace"—made Bob think of green pastures, still waters, and lying down to blessed sleep, but surely Jesus didn't think that Bob would have been up half the night if peace were anywhere in the offing.

Before Bob could restart his litany of concerns, Jesus held up a hand, as if to say, "Hold on a minute, friend." Jesus shrugged off his linen, outer robe, and then he took off a leather pack that had been slung across his back. Jesus shook back the pack's flap and loosened the drawstring at the top. He turned it upside down and gave it a shake, chasing out a dust bunny, a gum wrapper, and a stray penny. Then, with a hopeful expression, Jesus put the open bag right there in front of Bob.

"What's that?" Bob wanted to know.

"It's for your troubles, Bob. Go ahead. Just put them all in there, one by one." Bob eyed the leather pack. It looked about the size of a child's backpack. It had a bright yellow SpongeBob SquarePants sticker on the flap, and someone had plastered a tattered bumper sticker across its bulging midsection that said "Visualize Whirled Peas." The pack had the sort of worn, buttery look that comes to well-tanned leather when it sees plenty of use.

Feeling just a little condescended to, Bob started in, "Believe me, Jesus, there's no way all my troubles will fit in there."

But the Lord only smiled all the more and held out the sack. "C'mon, Bob. What have you got to lose? Give it a try." So Bob did.

He started with Maybelle Howard, and to his surprise both Maybelle and her walker fit into the pack, even though they were obviously much larger than it was. Next, Molly Hall and her mission trip crew hopped on in. Then Bob managed to shove the church's broken industrial fridge, the entire ladies auxiliary, a very pregnant Heather Rodriguez, and ten gallons of Hank Tinker's secret barbecue sauce into the bag. The pack swallowed everything up without complaint, although the tantalizing smell of warm barbecue sauce wafted up from its dark interior, making Bob's stomach growl. Bob soon realized that this was kind of fun. By the look of his grin, Jesus clearly thought that this was about as good as it gets. Bob kept going. There was room for the leaky toilet, the overflowing garbage, and the entire guest bedroom. Bob also packed up Paul's college plans and his personal retirement hopes. And then, for good measure, Bob handed Jesus Sparky's leash, trusting that if the Lord was willing to carry his troubles, then he could readily handle a late-night dog walk.

Bob looked at the pack, which by all means should have been bursting at the seams with all manner of people and problems, but the funny thing was that it didn't look any different than it had at the beginning. Bob couldn't be sure, but when Jesus snugged up the drawstring and buckled the flap, it looked like the SpongeBob SquarePants sticker sported an even bigger, goofier grin than before. Bob blinked.

"Feel better?" Jesus asked as he slung the pack over his shoulder as if it were completely weightless. Jesus wrapped his linen robe around his shoulders, and then he bent down and clipped the leash to Sparky's collar. The dog began to wriggle with excitement as if the thought of a late-night walk with Jesus was just about the best thing ever.

And Bob really did feel better. He felt light and loose and decidedly sleepy. "But Lord," Bob wanted to know, "How? Why? What?" His mind was too tired to even formulate a question.

Jesus smiled and shrugged. "Bob, I give you my peace. It's here whenever you need it. Don't let your heart be troubled."

And while Jesus held Bob's troubles and Sparky got his walk, Pastor Bob slept. He slept like a baby, or like a happy Labrador retriever after running up and down hills and barking at coyotes all night long, or like Marge, who has always had the coveted gift of untroubled sleep.

23

The Father's Love

"Now all the tax-collectors and sinners were coming near to
listen to him. And the Pharisees and the scribes were grumbling
and saying, 'This fellow welcomes sinners and eats with them.'
So he told them this parable."

—LUKE 15:1-3

Lenore Claiborne was standing in the checkout line at Green's Grocery
when she heard the news. She was so shocked that she forgot to put
back the *National Enquirer* that she was perusing. The checker had to ask
twice, "You gonna pay for that, Lenore, or what?"

Lenore loaded her groceries into the car and sat behind the wheel. She
was a large woman, prone to perspiring when anxious. The tickle of sweat
rolling down her back finally broke her reverie and prompted her to launch
the car in the direction of the church. If anyone could figure this out, it
would be Pastor Bob. If he didn't have any answers, she could at least get
him praying. He was good for that.

Lenore found Bob in the church office. He was trying to make copies,
but it didn't look like it was going so well. The side panel on the ancient
copier was open, three or four lights were flashing on the control panel, and
something smelled like it was burning. Lenore walked in, switched off the
machine, and took a seat. Pastor Bob, relieved to be temporarily distracted
from the copier, sat down, too. "Nice day, Lenore," he said.

Lenore shook her head. "Pastor Bob," she exclaimed, "we'll see how nice
you think it is once you've heard the news." Bob leaned forward, concerned
and expectant, and Lenore let him have it. "Scottie Tinker is back."

As a baby, Scottie had been baptized, right there in the Presbyterian Church. He had howled so loudly through the whole service that folks have been wearing earplugs on baptismal Sundays ever since. Later, when Scottie broke his father's heart, folks elbowed one another and exchanged meaningful looks, as if they should have known this was coming. That Scottie was a live wire. On cold winter mornings after a big snow, chances were good that you might catch him ditching school and thumbing his way down the Loj Road with his snowboard strapped to his back, ready to snowshoe up a mountain and surf on down. It's still considered a marvel that he had survived to graduate from high school.

Scottie was a natural in these mountains, and everyone anticipated that he would be an asset to the family business. The Tinkers had been outfitters since before the TB days. Scottie's dad Hank used to say that he couldn't wait for his two boys to take over the business, so he could spend all his time fishing with his buddies and perfecting his fly tying. But one day Scottie walked into the shop and told Hank he wanted out. His exact words were, "I'm done with you, Dad, and this crap town. Time to go."

What happened next—that was what *really* shocked people. Hank let Scottie go. In fact, Hank called up his broker and cashed in his life insurance. Next, he listed a prime chunk of lakefront property and sold it to some summer people for a pretty price. Then, Hank gave the boy enough money to do just about anything he wanted. The last anyone really knew of Scottie, he had purchased a round-the-world plane ticket and was bound for the airport in Montreal with just a backpack and his snowboard.

Over the years, stories trickled into town from time to time. Rumor had it that Scottie was spotted with a fast crowd at the Running of the Bulls in Pamplona. Once, Hank received a blank postcard from Nepal picturing jagged, towering mountains overshadowing a still, blue lake and terraced hills. One of Hank's wealthy downstate customers claimed she ran into Scottie coming down Mt. Kilimanjaro, and said, "Yeah, he was very skinny and had lost some teeth. His boots looked like they had seen better days, but it was him, alright."

Then the news stopped. Most people thought Scottie was dead—rolled in an alley, or overdosed, or caught up in an avalanche. It was only Hank who never lost hope that his younger son would one day come home. On summer evenings, Hank would sit out on the porch and wonder if things would have been different if Beth hadn't left when the boys were so little. He would smoke a cigar to keep the bugs at bay and listen for the sound of Scottie's boots crunching their way home down the gravel drive.

Jim, Hank's older son, had stepped up to shoulder all the business responsibilities. Jim was as solid as Scottie was wild. Although Jim had been baptized at the church, no one had found it particularly memorable. Jim had once played Joseph in the Christmas play, though, and folks had marveled at how right he was for the part—strong, quiet, humble! It was, of course, only a matter of time before Pastor Bob recruited Jim to serve as an elder, which he did with great faithfulness and humility. He was just that kind of guy.

Everyone knows that running your own business in the mountains is no picnic—especially when you are catering to folks from New Jersey who are hoping to have a wilderness adventure with all the comforts of home—but Jim never complained. He knew the best spots to catch fish, watch a sunset, spy shooting stars, or pick blueberries. Whether the man ever got a vacation was highly unlikely. It seemed he was always guiding trips, hauling gear, cleaning boats, selling boots, and coming to church on Sundays. If Hank Tinker had gotten a raw deal with Scottie as a son, he'd sure hit the jackpot with Jim.

If Hank never gave up hoping that Scottie would come home, it was hard to tell what Jim hoped. Whenever the subject of Scottie came up, Jim fell silent and took the first opportunity to make an exit. Folks knew what a heartache Scottie's disappearance had been for his dad, but no one ever gave much thought to what it must have meant for his big brother. It could not have been easy.

Now, Lenore Claiborne, pink and perspired with the stress of her news, sat in the church office and told Bob that the unthinkable had happened. "Scottie Tinker is alive! He's on his way home!"

A park ranger had spotted him, primitive camping on state land over by the Fulton Chain of Lakes. According to the ranger, Scottie had dreadlocks and was, indeed, missing his front teeth. He even had a big tattoo on his face. He also smelled pretty bad. It sounded like Scottie had had a change of heart after all these years, perhaps prompted more by his poverty than anything else. Scottie was making his way back to his hometown, hoping to do some guided trips for his dad when he arrived. Maybe, in time, he could even work his way back into Hank's good graces. If not, maybe Peter Bernard would take him on for guided excursions. If all else failed, Peter's son Franco would take him in at the On Belay Community. It seemed worth a shot, anyway.

Much to Lenore's annoyance, Pastor Bob listened to her bombshell with the same vague smile and appreciative nods that he demonstrated when she was filling him in on her newest recipes. "Pastor Bob, what is wrong with you?" Lenore asked when she was through with her report. "Aren't you gonna pick up the phone and call Hank?"

"No need to, Lenore," Bob answered. "He already knows. Came to see me at home, first thing this morning."

Pastor Bob seemed to think this was sufficient information. Lenore did not. Her anxiety mounting past the tipping point, she reached over to shake Bob's arm. "Pastor Bob! What is going to happen?"

Pastor Bob's smile got alarmingly large. "Well, Lenore, Hank's on his way to pick up Scottie, and we're going to have a humongous party." Bob walked over to the broken-down copier and extracted a flier from on top of the glass. In big, bold letters across the top, it said, "Welcome Home, Scottie!"

Lenore grabbed the flier and read it in disbelief. It seemed that Hank Tinker was planning a celebration after church next Sunday in the church hall—a pig roast! Church members were invited to bring side dishes or dessert, and there was even going to be some bluegrass music for folks to step lively. Lenore could not think of anything less appropriate. If Scottie Tinker were not a grown man, he would deserve a spanking for what he had put his father through, and here were Hank and Pastor Bob cooking up some big church picnic as if Scottie had just returned from Afghanistan.

"But Pastor Bob," Lenore stammered, "what does Jim have to say about it all?"

As if speaking to a very young child, Pastor Bob patted her hand and patiently explained, "Right now, Jim doesn't know. He's guiding a canoe trip out in the St. Regis Wilderness—no cell service. He'll be back on Saturday evening. I'm sure we'll see him in church on Sunday. Why don't you make some of your delicious coleslaw for the party?"

Lenore Claiborne couldn't think of another word to say, so she stood up to leave with the flier still clutched in her hand. She wasn't sure she was all that pleased that Scottie Tinker was back, and she had no intention of whipping up coleslaw on his behalf.

It didn't take long for the news to spread from one side of the village to the other. Come Sunday morning, the Presbyterian Church was so full that Ernie Leduc had to set up extra chairs, just like Christmas Eve. Lenore Claiborne was there, feeling annoyed that she had to share her favorite pew with visitors. She wasn't any more inclined to think Scottie deserved a welcome, but she did feel a certain obligation to support Hank. Early that morning, Maybelle Howard had called Lenore to report that Jim Tinker had arrived back from his guiding excursion. Apparently, he was not at all pleased with his little brother's resurrection appearance. Hank and Jim had quarreled right out in front of the shop, and Jim had driven off to spend the night in his truck.

Lenore looked around. There was Hank Tinker, in his usual pew near the front. Next to him, freshly showered, his dreadlocks pulled back into a ponytail and wearing his father's navy-blue blazer, was Scottie. The man looked so broken, and his father looked so happy and proud, that Lenore's heart melted. She felt embarrassed that she had begrudged Scottie his homecoming, and she was glad she had made her special coleslaw after all.

After the passing of the peace, Lenore saw Jim Tinker slip in. He appeared to be wearing the same paddling clothes that he had slept in. Jim's hair was stiff with bug dope. His typically clean-shaven face was shadowed with the beginnings of a beard. When he took off his sunglasses, he looked like he had had a very bad night. Jim did not sit with his father and Scottie, taking a seat instead on one of the extra chairs near the door to the narthex, as if ready to bolt at a moment's notice.

Lenore didn't think it likely that anyone heard a word of what Pastor Bob had to preach that morning. Everyone was too spellbound by the Tinker family drama. For his part, Bob did his best to convey the enormity of God's love for us—a limitless and unconditional gift that we don't deserve, and still God gives it, with no strings attached. "It's when we begin to accept God's amazing love for us," Bob preached, "that we begin to forge the capacity to selflessly love others. We learn to love the self-consumed prodigal, and the self-righteous neighbor, and on a good day, we even find the wherewithal to love ourselves." When Bob finished, only Hank Tinker said "Amen!"

It wasn't until the prayers of the people that something shifted in the sanctuary. As Pastor Bob asked folks to share their joys and concerns, Hank Tinker stood up. Now, in forty years of church membership, Hank had never said a word in worship, but there he was, swaying a little bit and gripping the back of the pew in front of him for support.

"Hank?" Pastor Bob said expectantly while the entire assembly held their collective breath.

"Pastor Bob," Hank began, "I'd like to thank God for the gift of my sons." Lenore noticed that both Scottie, at his father's side, and Jim, way in the back, looked down.

Hank placed a hand on Scottie's thin shoulder, "This son of mine was dead and has come to life; he was lost and has been found. I love him!" Scottie was crying now. His face tattoo was all crinkled up and his mouth was open wide so everyone could see where his teeth were missing.

"And this son of mine," now Hank had turned around to find Jim, "this son has been my rock and my right hand. How could I have ever made it through these hard years without him? I love him." Now Jim was crying, too, tears falling onto the front of his vest.

Hank continued, "I hope you *all* will join me after worship for a big celebration."

Now everyone was crying. Pastor Bob found his voice and spoke up, "Thanks be to God for the gift of sons—and thanks be to God for the greatness of a father's love. Party later. Who's coming?" The whole sanctuary broke into cheers and applause.

They are still telling stories about Scottie Tinker's celebration. Lenore Claiborne kicked up her heels and danced herself silly. Every bite of that roast pig? Eaten! Scottie and Jim Tinker let bygones be bygones. They shared an awkward man-hug, and even pulled their father into the embrace. No one had more fun at the party than Pastor Bob. After Lenore Claiborne had wheeled him around the dance floor a time or two, they caught their breath by the punchbowl. Lenore was tapping her feet and looking for her next dance victim.

"Well, Lenore," Bob asked, "how are you feeling about this party now?"

Lenore laughed, "Pastor Bob, I guess that if Hank Tinker can find it in his heart to love both those boys after what he has been through, I might as well try my best to do the same." Lenore winked at Bob, then trotted off to lay claim to her husband Steve, pulling him out onto the dance floor with an enthusiasm that overcame his reluctance.

Pastor Bob stood by the punchbowl and smiled. He figured that in all his years of parish ministry, this was the closest he had ever come to the kingdom of heaven.

24

The Vineyard

"They sow fields, and plant vineyards, and get a fruitful yield.
By his blessing they multiply greatly."

—Psalm 107:37-38A

"We think it should be called The Vineyard," Tubby Mitchell said, as he and Irene finished their presentation.

Pastor Bob cast an appraising eye around the session table, measuring how elders had received the vision that the Mitchells had cast for the future of the Burns property. A few looked bored. The deep furrow across Eugenia Bergstrom's brow told Bob that she was working to take it all in and form an opinion. The big smile on Heather Rodriguez's face clearly said that she was all for it. Tommy Stewart's face—jaw clamped, skin flushed—made Bob feel worried.

Bob sat up straighter, pushed his glasses up on his nose, and cleared his throat, but before he could thank the Mitchells, Tommy sputtered, "C'mon, folks. Really? Have you thought about this? There's no way it's going to work."

To be honest, Bob, too, had struggled to accept the idea when he had heard it just the month before in the pastor's study. "We've got an idea, Bob," Irene had started. "About Ethel Burns's place," Tubby had finished. Irene had continued, "Bob, we've got a nest egg. When our son was born, we began saving to help him buy his first home."

"Ahh," Bob murmured, remembering their son with a heavy heart. One of the best and brightest young men of his generation, Todd Mitchell had been killed by an IED in Iraq. Todd's was by far the toughest funeral that Bob had ever preached, struggling to keep the tears at bay as he began the service, "I am the resurrection and the life, says the Lord."

Irene continued, tears now filling her eyes, "When Todd didn't come home, we just continued to save. Maybe it was habit, maybe we couldn't accept that he would never have a home and a family and a future."

Tubby reached a reassuring arm around his wife's shoulders. She took a big breath, dabbed at her eyes, and finished in a rush, "We want to do something with that money, Bob, something to honor our boy."

As Irene's tears began to fall, Tubby spoke up. "Bob, we've got $80,000, and we believe the Lord is calling our church to do something with the Burns property."

Now, the Burns property had been the cause of a number of sleepless nights for Bob, ever since Ethel Burns had died and left it to the church. The house and ten-acre parcel adjacent to the churchyard was one of the oldest properties in town. In fact, more than 150 years earlier, Ethel's ancestors had donated the land on which the Presbyterian Church had been built.

At first, Bob and the session had been thrilled by the unexpected and generous bequest, but when they ventured behind the imposing stone walls that ringed the Burns property, they were overwhelmed by a nightmare of deferred maintenance. The furnace was a seventy-five-year-old, coal-burning monster that took up half the basement. The wiring had been completed sometime early in the last century and never improved. The old copper roof leaked and needed replacement. The plumbing had never been hooked up to the village's water, because Ethel had insisted that her well had the best water in town.

It wasn't just the house that needed help. Dead elms soared like gaunt stick figures above the wooded portion of the immense lot. Deadfall littered the undergrowth. The grass looked more like a hayfield than a lawn. Ethel's garden with its central arbor, where she had grown prized Concord grapes, was a wild, overgrown mass of weeds, vines, and brambles.

Six years since receiving the bequest, the session was still deadlocked over what to do. Sell, renovate, bulldoze? Overwhelmed and out of vision, they had drained the pipes and locked the doors. The garage had become a handy storage space for the church's riding mower. In the spring, Mr. Rosen would unlock the iron gates and take the pre-school children for a walk behind the walls to see the lady slippers that bloomed at the edge of the wood. In warm weather, Ernie Leduc, the church's sexton, would fire up the riding mower and crop the hay into something that resembled a lawn.

In late summer, the neighborhood kids would jump the walls to feast on Ethel's grapes, so sweet and delicious that the juice would run down their chins and stain their shirts.

Tubby and Irene envisioned transforming the Burns property into a place of joy and refreshment for the whole community. Clean out the woods and put in some walking trails. Take down the house and expand the garden. Keep the grape arbor, and add benches and gravel walks. Turn the large lawn into a playing field in the warm months, with a ring that could be flooded to freeze for skating in winter. To make the park more accessible, portions of the stone wall and the iron gates would come down. Finally, the salvaged stones and wrought iron would be forged into a columbarium, a memorial wall where church members could one day have their ashes interred.

As Tubby and Irene finished describing their beautiful vision to Pastor Bob that afternoon in his study, he could almost see it. But the thought of the effort it would take to achieve the dream gave Bob a feeling of achy tiredness. So much to do, and so few workers willing to head into the vineyard. It was tempting to thank Tubby and Irene and tell them to hold onto their money, but ever since Bob's brush with burnout, he had resolved to never again quench the spirit of his people's initiative, no matter how improbable their suggestions were. Things might get a little offbeat from time to time, but Bob figured it was better to harness that energy and get people involved than to pull the yoke of leadership alone.

Yet, as Bob sat at the session table across from the red-faced Tommy Stewart, who sputtered about liability, expense, ongoing maintenance, juvenile delinquents smoking weed, and homeless vagrants sleeping on benches, Bob began to doubt the wisdom of his decision. Maybe this idea should have been nipped in the bud. Bob's heart hurt for Tubby and Irene, their faces frozen in a wooden, panicked look as Tommy systematically undermined all their plans to honor their boy's memory and Ethel's legacy through the creation of a community park.

The dream might have ended right then if Eugenia, who had recently stepped up to serve as elder and proven to be every bit as formidable as Tommy, hadn't spoken. Every eye turned to look as she said with a faraway voice, "It's been years since I tasted Ethel's grapes. Every summer she hosted the ladies auxiliary for a garden party—cucumber sandwiches with the crust cut off, petit fours, and thimble-sized glasses of sherry. Oh, it was so lovely." For a moment, Tommy's resolve wavered as he remembered his mother, all those years ago, returning home from the ladies auxiliary summer picnic with a sweet and rosy glow.

Eugenia placed her hands palms down on the table in a gesture that spoke of resolve and unwritten authority. "It seems to me that the past should bless the future. I'm not getting any younger. I wouldn't mind my ashes resting in a place where folks can sit and pray. I like the thought of children skating, playing ball, and eating their fill of grapes. Let's make it happen."

Before Tommy could rebut Eugenia's remarks, Heather spoke up, "I love the idea of creating a place for my children to delight in God's world. I'm already thinking about a vacation bible school campout. How about a church picnic? I can't wait to take the twins next door and teach them how to skate." After that, the floodgates opened, with others imagining how the old Burns place could be a gift, not only for the church but also for their neighbors. But Tommy turned an alarming shade of red, looking increasingly apoplectic.

Eventually, Bob called the discussion to a close. "My friends, the Lord is calling us to work in 'The Vineyard.' Do we have a motion? Who wants to second that? All in favor, say, 'Aye.'" By a vote of eight to one, the session voted to accept the Mitchell's gift and embrace their vision.

It took eighteen months and countless volunteer hours for the church to transform Ethel Burns' place into The Vineyard. Chris Nelson recruited an arborist friend to take down those massive elms. He did it for free, hauling away all that prime firewood. José Rodriguez sent over a driver with a backhoe and front end loader from the quarry. He spent days painstakingly grading the yard for the playing field. Then, Heather taught a Sunday school lesson on the Parable of the Sower and got the kids to scatter grass seed. Eugenia Bergstrom organized a search committee to find a sculptor who would transform their salvaged stones and iron into a memorial wall and columbarium. Irene Mitchell led the charge in taming the grapes, patiently pruning back the overgrowth, rebuilding the arbor, and fertilizing the soil. Slowly, the Mitchell's vision began to become a reality.

It wasn't until it was time to take the old house down that Tommy Stewart had a change of heart. He caught up to Bob one Saturday morning in the woodland as Bob tied bits of bright flagging to trees to lay out a walking path. "Hey, Bob, I've been thinking about the house," Tommy began. Bob paused, wondering what new argument Tommy had developed to halt their progress, but Tommy seemed to have a new spirit. "Have you talked to a salvage company? Ethel's deferred maintenance could be to our advantage. Do you have any idea what those yuppies downstate will pay for a clawfoot tub or a tin ceiling? Let me make some calls." And so, Tommy, who had been so opposed to The Vineyard, joined the workers.

Tommy found a scrap-metal broker who harvested the copper roof and plumbing and cut the church in on the profits of the sale. He retained an architectural salvage company that took away not only the bathtubs and tin ceiling but also the windows, doors, floors, sinks, commodes, radiators, and lighting fixtures. When it came to the actual demolition, there had been very little left to do but push what was left of the house into the cavernous basement with the coal-burning furnace. Like an enormous grave, they covered it all with a generous earthen berm.

The final touch on the project was a sign, painted by Heather and the church's children. It read, in big, crooked letters, "The Vineyard." Purple grapes and curlicue vines snaked around the border. On the Sunday when Pastor Bob led his flock out of the sanctuary and through the stone walls of the Burns property to dedicate the columbarium, he was inundated with requests from church members to purchase niches so that their ashes might one day rest on church property.

One evening as Bob was leaving the church, he looked over to The Vineyard and saw the Mitchells, resting on a bench in the garden. As he walked over to join them, he could smell the heavy fragrance of the arbor in bloom and hear the droning of countless bees, swarming the blossoms. Bob took a seat on the bench next to Tubby and Irene, watching with wonder the great dance of life surging around Ethel's grapes. Past the arbor, Bob could see the swell of the earthen berm. There, Tommy and his wife Kitten were patiently planting perennials—coneflowers, lilies, irises, and columbine—that would one day ripple across the berm in a bright tide. The sound of a ball being kicked made Bob turn to look at the field where neighborhood kids were playing soccer. At the edge of the woods, Bob could see Eugenia Bergstrom and her pug, Calvin, out for their evening walk. Bob took a deep breath and felt a surge of gratitude that started at the tips of his toes and rocketed right up to the top of his head. He was overcome by the goodness and the blessing of what had been forged from the memory of a lost son and the legacy of a thrifty saint.

After a while, Bob's stomach rumbled. He rose and gave Tubby's shoulder a pat. He nodded to Irene. "I'm so glad, my friends, that the Lord called you to work in the vineyard." The bees buzzed, the kids called for a penalty kick, Eugenia bent down to pick up after her dog, and Bob walked off in anticipation of Marge's good cooking.

CPSIA information can be obtained
at www.ICGtesting.com
Printed in the USA
BVHW091314240621
609862BV00004B/17